Meets Father Christmas
and Other Stories

Joan G. Robinson was trained as an illustrator and began writing her own stories in 1939. Over thirty of her books were published before her death in 1988. Her most enduring character, Teddy Robinson, first appeared in 1953. This collection of stories has been selected by the author's daughter Deborah – star of the books and owner of the real Teddy Robinson.

Books by Joan G. Robinson from
Macmillan Children's Books

The Teddy Robinson Storybook

Teddy Robinson Meets Father Christmas
and Other Stories

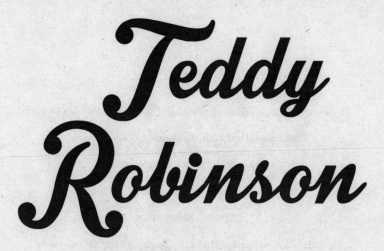

Teddy Robinson

Meets Father Christmas

and Other Stories

Joan G. Robinson

MACMILLAN CHILDREN'S BOOKS

The stories in this collection were first published by George G. Harrap & Co. Ltd

This edition published 2017 by Macmillan Children's Books
an imprint of Pan Macmillan
20 New Wharf Road, London N1 9RR
Associated companies throughout the world
www.panmacmillan.com

ISBN 978-1-5098-0613-3

1 3 5 7 9 8 6 4 2

A CIP catalogue record for this book is available from the British Library.

Printed and bound by CPI Group (UK) Ltd, Croydon CR0 4YY

For Gregory and Barnaby and
all Families with a Teddy Bear

Contents

1

Teddy Robinson Meets
Father Christmas

One day Teddy Robinson looked out of Deborah's window and saw that all the trees were quite bare and there was a little pattern of frost on the window-pane.

"I suppose this is winter-time," he said. "Br-r-r-r! I'm glad I've got a fur coat."

"Yes," said Deborah, "it's winter-time, and it's nearly Christmas. Shall I sing you a Christmas carol?"

"Yes, please," said Teddy Robinson. So Deborah sang him the *Rocking Carol*, which begins like this:

"Little Jesus, sweetly sleep, do not stir,
We will lend a coat of fur.
We will rock you, rock you, rock you."

"I like that," said Teddy Robinson. He thought the words were very pretty and wished he could have been there to lend his own coat of fur.

Then Deborah told him all about Father Christmas, and how he would come and fill their stockings with toys on Christmas night.

"We must hang up a stocking for you, Teddy Robinson," she said. "I specially want a paint-box in mine. What do you specially want in yours?"

"I don't specially want anything," said Teddy Robinson, "except to see Father Christmas when he comes. We shall see him, shan't we?"

"No, I don't think so," said Deborah. "Mummy says he never comes unless every one is asleep."

"But I did see him once, didn't I?" said Teddy Robinson.

"No, you couldn't have," said Deborah.

"But I did. I'm sure I did. At least, I think I did. Are you sure I didn't?"

"I don't think you could have," said Deborah.

"Oh," said Teddy Robinson, "then I must have dreamt it." But he still didn't quite believe it.

For the next few days they were very busy making Christmas cards, and choosing presents for people, and learning Christmas carols, and helping to put up the decorations.

Teddy Robinson wasn't very good at learning the carols. Deborah tried to teach him *Good King Wenceslas*, but he got it wrong every time.

"Try again," said Deborah.

Teddy Robinson sat up very straight and sang, "Goofing Wempers Lass Look-out . . ."

"No!" said Deborah. "That's *wrong*."

"Well, I think I'm better at making up my own songs," said Teddy Robinson. "I'll sing it my own way.

> "Teddy Robin-son look-out
> On the feast of Stephen,
> All the stars were round about,
> Some odd ones and some even."

"No, that won't do at all," said Deborah. "I think we'd better go and help Daddy and Mummy with the decorations."

So they did; and after that Deborah went off to

3

wrap up her Christmas presents and hide them in a secret place.

Teddy Robinson hadn't any presents for anyone, but he was very busy making up a Christmas song which he was going to sing to Deborah on Christmas morning. So far he had only made up half of it, and when he couldn't think of the right words he just sang te-tumty-tum to fill in the spaces. It went something like this:

"Hooray, hooray,
it's Christmas Day,
your stocking's full already.
Te-tumty-tum, te-tumty-tum,
with lots of love from Teddy."

It's a good idea for a present, he thought, because I don't have to buy it, and I don't have to wrap it up and hide it away; I just make it up in my head and keep it there until Christmas Day. I hope I get it finished in time, he said to himself.

At last it was Christmas Eve. When bed-time

came Deborah and Teddy Robinson hung up their stockings side by side. Deborah's was one of her long winter socks, and Teddy Robinson's was one of his little blue bootees.

They hung up their stockings
side by side

"We must go to sleep quickly to-night," said Deborah, "because it's a magic night."

So they snuggled down together and lay and thought about Christmas until Deborah fell asleep, and then Teddy Robinson lay and thought about Christmas all by himself.

Much later on Mummy came in quietly to see if Deborah was asleep. She lifted Teddy Robinson out of the bed, kissed him softly on the nose, and then sat him on the window-sill while she straightened the blankets and tucked Deborah up tidily.

Teddy Robinson was glad he had been put on the window-sill. Deborah had said it was a magic night, and he very much wanted to see what a magic night looked like.

When Mummy had gone he peeped through the curtains and stared out into the darkness. A few lights were still burning in the upstairs windows of the houses near by, but most of the houses were dark because all the people had gone to bed. He watched until one by one the lights had all gone out, and then he stared up into the sky. The stars were there, twinkling and sparkling and winking, just as they had been on the night when he had slept out in the garden. He wondered if they could see him now, peeping through the curtains.

Then the clock in the church tower struck twelve, slowly and clearly. Teddy Robinson counted one, two, three, four, three times over; and then he held his breath and listened. Very faint and far away he thought he could hear the sound of tiny jingling bells.

At the same moment he noticed that the stars seemed to be twinkling much more brightly, and some of them were spinning round and round, and shooting across the sky, just as if something very exciting was happening up there. The noise of the jingling bells grew louder, as if it was coming nearer, until soon all the air seemed to be filled with the sound.

And as Teddy Robinson sat there watching the stars spinning and listening to the music of the bells ringing he suddenly remembered that he *had* seen Father Christmas. Long, long ago, when he was a new little teddy bear, it was Father Christmas who had brought him to Deborah's house. They had come swooping through the sky in a sleigh pulled by reindeer, and the stars had all to shoot out of their way because they were travelling so quickly, and the sleigh bells were all ringing just as they were now.

He began to feel excited and happy, and a little song began to make itself up in his head:

> Magic night,
> magic night,
> all the children tucked up tight.
> Father Christmas on his way,
> driving in his magic sleigh.
> Toys he brings,
> and dolls and things,
> and every silver sleigh bell rings,
> While down below a brown bear sings——

Before he could get any further a draught of cold air blew the curtains inward, and Teddy Robinson fell backward off the window-sill and rolled over on to his back on the carpet.

And there in the middle of the room stood Father Christmas!

Teddy Robinson was so surprised that he just lay on his back and stared. Father Christmas smiled, and picked him up, and laughed quietly as he stroked his ears.

"Hallo, Teddy Robinson," he said. "Did I give you a surprise? Do you remember me?"

"Yes, I do now," said Teddy Robinson. "You're Father Christmas, and you brought me here when I was new. I suddenly remembered when I heard the sleigh-bells ringing."

"That's right," said Father Christmas. "You were a new little bear then; I can see you are older now, but you still look just like Teddy Robinson. Are you happy here with Deborah?"

"Yes, very happy."

"Good," said Father Christmas. "I chose you for her because I knew she would love you. Do you remember the night I brought you here?"

"I only half remember it," said Teddy Robinson. "It seems like a dream I once had. Do tell me about it."

"All right," said Father Christmas, "but first I'd better fill Deborah's stocking."

"Have you brought her a paint-box?" asked Teddy Robinson.

"Yes, and I've brought her a drawing book and some pencils to go with it," said Father Christmas.

"That's good," said Teddy Robinson. "Her old ones are all blunt, and they're too short to draw with. What else have you brought her?"

"Oh, all sorts of little surprises," said Father Christmas, "but you'll have to wait till the morning to see them."

Then he opened his big sack and brought out a lot of little parcels all tied up in different coloured papers with gold and silver string, and he packed them into Deborah's stocking as tightly as they would go. When at last the stocking was full right up to the top he looked at Teddy Robinson's little blue bootee.

"That's mine," said Teddy Robinson, "but you don't have to put anything in it."

"No," said Father Christmas, "but I will, all the same. Promise not to look."

So Teddy Robinson promised and stared hard at the ceiling while Father Christmas filled his blue bootee with a string of beads, a lollipop, two pattypans, and a cracker.

Then he bent over to look at Deborah, kissed her gently on the cheek, and came back to Teddy Robinson.

"Now," he said, "I'll tell you all about the night I brought you here," and he sat down on the low chair by the window and took Teddy Robinson on his knee.

"It was Christmas night, of course," said Father Christmas, "and we started off with a sleigh full of toys. You were near the top of the sack because you specially wanted to be near a little toy horse called Cloppety——"

"Oh! I know him!" said Teddy Robinson. "I met him in hospital."

"Did you, now!" said Father Christmas. "I remember I was taking him to a little boy called Tommy."

"Yes, I know him as well," said Teddy Robinson.

"Fancy that!" said Father Christmas. "Well, that night we went so fast that the sack came undone and you nearly fell out. So I brought you out and tucked you inside my big red coat, with only your nose and eyes peeping out.

"We went rushing along, and the stars had to keep shooting out on either side of us to get out of our way, and you kept peeping out over the edge of my coat and saying, 'Oh, my! Oh, my! We *are* up high!' Dear me, you *did* enjoy that ride!"

"I bet I did," said Teddy Robinson, and he felt his fur tingling with excitement. "Go on telling me."

"There isn't much more to tell," said Father Christmas; "it was a long ride, and as we began to swoop down towards the earth you began to get sleepy. We passed over the tops of some fir-trees, I remember, and woke up some birds who were sleeping on a branch, and then we saw the roofs and chimney-pots of the first houses, and then, as you were only a very new little bear, you began to get sleepier and sleepier, and by the time we got here to Deborah's house you were sound asleep."

"I think I remember now," said Teddy Robinson. "I hope I don't forget again before next Christmas."

"I don't think you will," said Father Christmas,

"because I have got a present in my pocket that I think will just fit you, and I hope it will make you always remember me. Shall I give it you now, or shall I put it in your stocking?"

"I'd like it now, please," said Teddy Robinson.

So Father Christmas felt deep down in the big red pocket of his big red coat, and he brought out a beautiful little collar made of red leather with a shiny silver bell fastened on to the front of it.

"I made it myself," he said. "I was making some new reins for the reindeer, and when I had finished there was one little strip of leather left over, and one little silver bell, so I made it into a collar."

Then he fastened it round Teddy Robinson's neck and Teddy Robinson was so pleased that he hardly knew how to say thank you. Every time he shook his head the little bell tinkled.

"And now I must be off," said Father Christmas. "Lots and lots of empty stockings are waiting to be filled, and it's high time all teddy bears were asleep."

"Couldn't I come with you?" asked Teddy Robinson.

"What! And leave Deborah?" said Father Christmas.

"No, I suppose not," he said. "I was only thinking I *would* like another ride with you. Where is your sleigh now?"

"In the garden," said Father Christmas. "Now I

"Now hop into bed like a good bear"

must fly; so hop into bed like a good bear, and I'll tuck you up before I go."

"I haven't learned to hop yet," said Teddy Robinson.

"No, of course not," said Father Christmas, "and I haven't learned to fly. I only meant it's time for me to go, and time for you to be in bed."

Then very gently he tucked him in beside Deborah, whispered "Happy Christmas," and a moment later there was a jingling of bells, a soft swishing noise outside the window, and then everything was quiet. Father Christmas had gone.

Teddy Robinson lay in the dark and thought how lovely it would have been to have sent the stars spinning and to go rushing through the sky to the North Pole with the wind whistling through his fur, and the little silver bell on his collar ringing with all the sleigh bells.

But then he saw the knobbly shape of Deborah's stocking hanging by the bed, and the smaller knobbly shape of his own stocking hanging beside it. He felt the ends of Deborah's hair tickling his ears as he cuddled down beside her, and he knew that Father Christmas had been quite right to leave him there. He didn't ever want to live anywhere else in the world except in Deborah's house.

And that is the end of the story about how
Teddy Robinson met Father Christmas.

2

Teddy Robinson
in Disguise

One day Teddy Robinson was sitting by a garden pool looking at the water-lilies when a toad suddenly slipped out of the water and scrambled up the bank. He sat by the edge of the pool and looked up at Teddy Robinson with tiny, bright eyes that shone like jewels.

"Hallo," said Teddy Robinson, "who are you?"

"I am a prince in disguise," croaked the toad.

"What does that mean?" said Teddy Robinson.

"It means I look like a toad, but I'm really a prince."

"Is that true?" asked Teddy Robinson.

"I hope so," said the toad. "It's the story I've always told."

"It's a very nice story," said Teddy Robinson. "I wish I could think of one like that."

"And who are you?" asked the toad.

"I am a prince in disguise"

Teddy Robinson thought quickly.

"I am a horse in disguise," he said.

"You don't look like one," said the toad.

"Nor do you look like a prince," said Teddy Robinson.

"I never talk to rude people," said the toad, and dived into the pool again.

Teddy Robinson had not meant to be rude and thought it rather silly of the toad to be so touchy, but he didn't mind. He went on staring at the water-lilies and thinking about what the toad had told him. He decided it would be rather jolly to be some one in disguise.

Later on, when he was at home again, Teddy Robinson practised standing on four legs on the toy-cupboard.

"Whatever are you doing?" said Deborah.

"Who do you think I am?" said Teddy Robinson.

"Who do you think I am?"

"You're my funny old bear standing on four legs. Why?"

"Oh," said Teddy Robinson. "I was rather hoping

19

you would think I was the milkman's horse."

"But why should I?" said Deborah. "You don't *look* like a horse."

A little later Teddy Robinson called to Deborah again. This time he was lying on his tummy with his paws stretched out in front of him.

"Who am I now?" he asked. "You can see I'm swimming."

"A bear at the seaside?" said Deborah.

"No. A fish," said Teddy Robinson crossly. "You don't seem to know a disguise when you see one."

"But I don't see one," said Deborah. "You have to *look* like some one if you're in disguise. It's no good just acting like some one. I'll show you one day, but not now. Andrew is coming and he's bringing Spotty, his toy dog."

Teddy Robinson growled. "*Must* they come? I don't like Spotty. He argues too much. Can't we be out?"

"No. I've said we'll be in," said Deborah. "Andrew thought Spotty would be nice company for you."

"I don't want company," said Teddy Robinson. "I want to be alone."

"I didn't know you'd mind, or I wouldn't have asked them," said Deborah. "But we can't stop them now, can we?"

Teddy Robinson began thinking hard. "Tell them we've moved," he said. "Let's move house before they come."

"That would be too difficult," said Deborah.

"Let's move ourselves, then," said Teddy Robinson. "Let's go away."

"We can't. I said we'd be here."

"Then let's think of some way to make them go past the house," said Teddy Robinson. "I know! Let's chalk arrows on the pavement going right on up the road."

"But where would the arrows go to?" said Deborah.

They both thought hard about this. Then Teddy Robinson said, "I know! Let the arrows go down the little hill into the pond. They'd be sure to follow them. People always follow arrows."

21

"They'd get very wet," said Deborah.

"We could write STOP HERE just by the railing," said Teddy Robinson.

"Yes, that's true," said Deborah.

"And we could leave them a little stool to sit on, and a book to read," said Teddy Robinson kindly. "Then they could stay there till it was time for them to go home again."

"So they could," said Deborah.

"Quick, get the chalk!" said Teddy Robinson.

So Deborah found the chalk and her little stool and a picture book, and put them all together in a paper carrier bag.

But at that moment the door-bell rang.

"Goodness, we're too late!" said Deborah. "Here they are!"

"Hide me," said Teddy Robinson. "Oh, how I wish I were in disguise!"

Deborah emptied the things out of the carrier bag.

"Here you are," she said. "This will do for a disguise." And she slipped the bag over his head.

"But who am I meant to be?" said Teddy Robinson.

Deborah read the printing on the bag.

"It says: 'Smith and Son, High-class Groceries, Family Business,' " she said. "You'd better be that."

She slipped her Wellington boots over his feet.

"Now you are quite covered up," she said. And at that moment the door opened and Andrew and Spotty came in.

"Didn't you hear the door-bell?" asked Andrew. "Your mummy let us in. I was afraid you weren't here."

"Teddy Robinson isn't," said a deep, growly voice from under the carrier bag.

"Where is he, then?" said Spotty.

Deborah said, "I'm afraid you won't see him today. He's gone into business."

"I don't know what that means exactly," said Andrew.

"Nor do I," said Deborah, "but that's where Teddy Robinson's gone."

"Who's that, then?" said Spotty, staring hard at the bag.

"That's Smith and Son," said Deborah.

"I don't believe it," said Spotty.

"All right, then—read it and see," said the deep growly voice from under the bag.

"I can't—it's upside down," said Spotty.

"Huh! Some people can't even read things upside down!" said the growly voice.

"And *some* people can't even read things the right way up," said Spotty. "Teddy Robinson can't, for one."

Teddy Robinson nearly shouted, "I can!— short words, anyway," but he remembered just in time and said, "I'm Mr Smith and Son, High-class Groceries—that's who I am."

"I don't believe it," said Spotty again.

Andrew lifted him on to the stool beside Teddy Robinson, and Spotty peered over the top of the carrier bag to spell out the writing.

"Smith and Son—so it is!" he said. "But I still don't believe it."

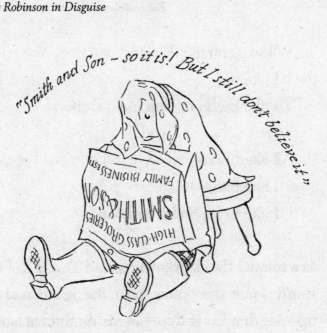

"Smith and Son – so it is! But I still don't believe it"

"Don't believe what?" said Deborah.

"What it says on the bag," said Spotty.

"Well, it's silly to argue all day," said Deborah. "Let's go out for a walk."

So Deborah, Andrew, and Spotty all went out, and Teddy Robinson stayed sitting on the cupboard under the bag.

It was dark inside, and it smelt of bacon and coffee and all sorts of nice things mixed up together.

Teddy Robinson began singing a little song about it:

"I like coffee,
I like tea,
I like bacon in with me.

I like biscuit,
I like bun,
I like being Smith and Son."

In a minute the door opened, and Teddy Robinson heard some one come into the room and start opening drawers and cupboards. A moment later the bag was lifted off his head, and there was Mummy smiling at him with her arms full of clothes.

"Whatever are you doing there?" she said, laughing; and, tucking him under her arm, she carried him into the kitchen with the carrier bag and the bundle of clothes.

"Here we are," said Mummy, putting them all down on the table. "I've found quite a lot of things that are too small for Deborah now. I shall be glad if you can use them for Marlene, and here is a bag to put them in."

Teddy Robinson looked round and saw that Mummy was talking to Mrs White, who sometimes came to help with the cleaning. She was sitting at the table with her little girl, Marlene, on her lap.

Mummy and Mrs White began sorting out the clothes and holding them up against Marlene to see if they fitted.

"Oh, here is one of Debbie's first baby dresses!" said Mummy, "and the little bonnet that went with it. These are too small even for Marlene. I should think they would just fit Teddy Robinson."

She put the dress on him, tied the bonnet under his chin, and wrapped him in an old baby-shawl. Then she held him out to Marlene.

"There you are," she said, "there's a baby for you."

Oh, dear! thought Teddy Robinson, I hope I'm not being given away.

But Mummy said, "Not to keep; only to play with while we're talking. We couldn't give Teddy Robinson away."

Marlene hugged him tightly and toddled out of the back door. Her own push-chair was waiting outside. She sat Teddy Robinson in it, then pushed him along to the garden, and there she wheeled him happily round and round the lawn.

Teddy Robinson was happy too. It was great fun to be disguised as a very small baby when he was really a middling-sized, middle-aged bear. He began singing:

> "Round and round the garden
> like a teddy bear———"

then he suddenly remembered he wasn't like a teddy bear at all—he was like a baby, so he changed it to:

> "Round and round the garden
> in the open air,
> looking like a baby,
> *not* a teddy bear . . ."

When Mummy called Marlene in to have some tea Teddy Robinson stayed sitting in the push-chair in the garden. Soon he heard voices and guessed that Deborah, Andrew, and Spotty were coming back from their walk. He couldn't see, because he had his back to the house, but it sounded as if Spotty was still arguing.

"—it depends what you mean by *high-class* groceries," he was saying. "How do we know they were? You can't believe everything you see written on a paper bag."

"Oh, Spotty, do stop!" said Deborah in a tired voice. "You've talked about nothing else the whole afternoon."

Teddy Robinson laughed to himself under the baby's bonnet.

"I always said he argued too much," he said to himself, and was glad to think he had missed the walk with Spotty.

The front gate banged, and he heard footsteps coming down the side path towards the back door. Suddenly they stopped, and he heard Deborah's voice say, "Hallo! There's a strange baby in our garden. We must have got visitors."

...laughed to himself under the baby's bonnet

"Bother," said Andrew. "I suppose we'd better go, then."

"I hate babies," said Spotty.

"I rather like them," said Deborah. "Wait here a minute and I'll see who it is."

She ran up to the push-chair, and Teddy Robinson nearly laughed out loud when he saw her surprised face.

"It's *you*!" she said, "I thought you were a real baby!"

"Hush!" said Teddy Robinson. "Don't tell them it's me. Have they gone yet?"

Deborah looked round. "Not yet," she said.

"I'll soon make them go," said Teddy Robinson, and he began making a noise like a baby crying—a cross, tired, whining baby.

"That's why I hate babies," said Spotty to Andrew. "They're boring. Let's go."

Deborah looked round again.

"Yes, this *is* rather a boring baby," she said. "It looks as if it's going to go on crying for a long while, too. Perhaps you had better go home."

"All right. Good-bye," said Andrew.

Just then Spotty caught sight of the carrier bag that Mrs White had put out on the back step, ready to take home.

"*There* you are!" he said. "Smith and Son, High-class Groceries. And they're not high-class groceries at all; they're old clothes! I *said* you couldn't believe what you saw written on a bag. I *said* it all depended what you meant by . . ."

Andrew carried him away still arguing.

Deborah laughed and hugged Teddy Robinson.

"That *was* a good disguise!" she said. "However did you do it?"

"Oh, it was quite easy," said Teddy Robinson. "I'm getting rather good at disguises now, aren't I? Do you remember ages ago, when I was quite a young bear, how I thought I could look like a horse by just standing on four legs?"

"Yes," said Deborah. "But that wasn't ages ago— that was only this afternoon."

"Was it really?" said Teddy Robinson. "Well, it seems ages ago to me. I've had quite a lot of fun since then."

And that is the end of the story about
Teddy Robinson in disguise.

3

Teddy Robinson Goes
to the Dolls' Hospital

One day Teddy Robinson was waving good-bye to Daddy when he waved so hard that all of a sudden his arm came right off.

"Oh, my goodness," he said, very surprised to see his arm in Deborah's hand without the rest of him joined on to it, "I seem to be going all to pieces."

"Never mind, my poor boy," said Deborah; "Mummy will mend it."

But Mummy said she could only sew it on, and then it wouldn't be able to swivel round any more.

"And what's the good of that?" said Teddy Robinson. "I *must* have an arm that swivels round." And he was so set on it that Mummy said he had better go to the Dolls' Hospital.

So off they went to the toyshop, which was also the Dolls' Hospital. Teddy Robinson was so pleased to be going that he sang all the way there, and Deborah hardly had a chance to remind him about saying please and thank you, and not showing off, and not singing too loudly in the middle of the night.

The man in the Dolls' Hospital said yes, he could mend Teddy Robinson's arm and they could fetch him again on Friday.

"This is his nightie," said Deborah, handing a little bag over the counter, "and when are visiting days, please?"

"Oh, dear," said the man; "I don't usually have visiting days. People just come when it's time to fetch them again."

"— and when are visiting days, please?"

Deborah was rather disappointed. She had hoped she would be able to see all the dolls in their little cots and beds.

"It doesn't seem fair," she said. "He came with me when I went to hospital."

But the man promised to take good care of him, and as he looked the sort of man who understood teddy bears, Deborah decided not to mind and kissed Teddy Robinson good-bye.

After that he was taken into a room behind the shop where all the other animals and dolls were waiting to be mended. The man put him up on the top shelf between a stuffed horse and a felt cat; then he went back to the shop.

The stuffed horse looked at Teddy Robinson. He lowered his head; his legs slipped out sideways.

"Horsey's the name," he said. "How do you do? No need to ask why you're here—I see you've lost an arm, poor fellow."

"Oh, no, I haven't lost it," said Teddy Robinson; "I've brought it with me. It just needs fixing on again."

"My trouble's of long standing," said the horse. "You see, it's my legs. They slide out sideways and then I fall on my nose. I'm hoping to get new wires put in them."

"My trouble's of long standing"

The felt cat stared hard at Teddy Robinson as if she wanted to be noticed. He smiled politely.

"I hope you are not here for anything serious?" he asked.

"It's my insides," said the cat, smiling proudly. "My squeak is worn out. They're going to put a new one in, *if* they can, which I very much doubt." She purred softly. "I'm not at all an easy case."

"Oh, I'm sorry," said Teddy Robinson.

"*I* don't mind," said the cat. "It's very interesting.

36

Makes something to talk about. I like coming here."

"Have you been here before, then?"

"Oh, yes, often. There's nothing I haven't had done—new ears, new eyes, re-stuffing, everything."

"Fancy that," said Teddy Robinson, "and I thought I was quite important coming only once."

The dolls all made quite a fuss of Teddy Robinson because he was the only teddy bear there. They called him Teddy right from the start, so he decided not to bother about his second name as he didn't want to make himself seem more special than anyone else.

And then the Other Bear arrived. He was a new-looking bear with golden-yellow fur, and when he was brought in all the dolls said, "Oooh, what a handsome teddy bear! Shall we call him Goldie?"

But the Other Bear said, "No, thank you. I prefer to be called by my own name. It is rather a distinguished one." He then bowed slightly from the waist, looking very proud and handsome, and said, "You may call me Teddy Robinson."

"Hi!" called Teddy Robinson from the top shelf,

"you can't do that. It's my name."

"Oh, no," said the felt cat, "you can't have it too. He thought of it first—a most distinguished name."

"You can have Brown for a second name," said one of the dolls kindly. "It will suit you."

So from then on Teddy Robinson was called Teddy Brown, and the Other Bear was called Teddy Robinson, which made the real Teddy Robinson very cross indeed.

The dolls made as much fuss of the Other Bear as they had made of Teddy Robinson. He told them he was there because one of his legs was loose, although he was still almost new.

"I was expensive," he said, "so it should never have happened. I think it's because I've been shown off so much. I'm rather a special bear, you see. I'm told some one has even written a book about me."

"You *are* lucky to be such a Special bear," said the dolls.

"Oh, yes," said the Other Bear, "but I suppose we can't all be Special, and I expect even quite ordinary bears with names like Smith or Brown have people who are quite fond of them."

Just then the shop man came in, carrying a beautiful big doll. She was wearing a pink silk dress with a bonnet to match and she had a very pretty face. But her eyes were closed.

Teddy Robinson looked over the top shelf and saw that it was Jacqueline. Jacqueline was a doll he knew. She belonged to a little girl called Mary Anne who was a friend of Deborah. Teddy Robinson had always admired Jacqueline ever since she had come to his birthday party and laughed at all his jokes. Her eyes had been shut even then, but she had never stopped smiling all through the party.

The shop man laid Jacqueline down gently on the bottom shelf, next to the Other Bear, then he went out again.

"Oooh!" said all the dolls. "A Sleeping Beauty!"

Jacqueline smiled sweetly, then said, "Tell me, is my friend Teddy Robinson still in the hospital?"

"Why, yes!" they said, "he is right beside you."

Up on the top shelf the real Teddy Robinson was doing his best to fall at Jacqueline's feet and tell her that *he* was the real one.

"Stop pushing," said the horse. "You'll only upset everybody. We don't all want to fall off the shelf."

"But I know her!" said Teddy Robinson.

"Why all the fuss?" said the felt cat. "Can't somebody ask her if she knows Teddy Brown?"

"Teddy Brown?" said Jacqueline, "no, I've never heard of him."

"There you are, you see," said the felt cat, "she doesn't know you at all. It's Teddy Robinson she knows, and I'm not surprised—such a distinguished name. Now do sit quiet."

So poor Teddy Robinson had to sit tight while the others talked down below.

"I've come to have my eyes unstuck," he heard Jacqueline say. "They were shut even when I came to your party, do you remember?"

"No, I can't say I do," said the Other Bear, who, of course, hadn't been at Teddy Robinson's party at all.

"Who is that growling up there?" asked Jacqueline suddenly.

"Teddy Brown," said the dolls. "Take no notice."

"What a bad-tempered bear," said Jacqueline. Then she said to the Other Bear, smiling sweetly, "Don't you really remember me, Teddy Robinson?"

"No, I'm afraid not," said the Other Bear, "but of course I meet so many pretty dolls I could hardly remember them all."

"I never thought Teddy Robinson would forget me," said Jacqueline sadly. "I always remember him and how beautifully he sang."

"Yes," said the Other Bear, "I am told I have quite a good voice—a sort of bearitone," and he began making a sort of growling la-la-la noise.

"Are you *sure* you're Teddy Robinson?" said Jacqueline, looking puzzled. "You sound so different."

"Of course I'm sure," said the Other Bear.

"And yet," said Jacqueline, "Teddy Robinson used to make up proper songs, with his own words, not just la-la-la."

"All right, so can I," said the Other Bear, and after a lot of coughing and humming and ha-ing he sang:

"I—er—ah—um, here's a song
all about er—um—ah—um,
hear me sing—er—sing a song,
la-la-la-la tumty-tum."

"No," said Jacqueline, "you're not Teddy Robinson at all. I didn't think you could be. Teddy Robinson is not only the handsomest and cleverest bear I know. He is also the most modest. And he would never call *that* singing."

Up on the top shelf the real Teddy Robinson was thinking round and round in his head. He had been quite sure he was Teddy Robinson until he heard Jacqueline say what a bad-tempered bear he was. Then he began to wonder.

"How can I be sure I'm me?" he asked the horse quietly.

"Who else do you feel like?" said the horse in a horse whisper.

"Well, I'm not feeling quite myself," said Teddy Robinson, "but I thought it was having only one arm." He began singing softly:

"Am I me?
Or am I me?
And if I'm not,
who can I be?"

"I know that voice!" cried Jacqueline, down below.

"It's the silly bear on the top shelf," said the dolls.

"Do let him go on," said Jacqueline, and when Teddy Robinson heard this he knew that of course he was himself, even if he didn't *feel* quite himself, and he sang out at the top of his voice:

"Stick me up
or blow me down,
call me Smith
or call me Brown,
call me Jones
for all I care,
call me just a silly bear,
*but I'm still Teddy Robinson and
nobody else, so there!*"

And then, because he had no breath left, he over-balanced, and with a cry of "Jacqueline!" he fell at her feet with a bump.

"Jacqueline!" he cried, and fell at her feet

"Oh, my dear Teddy Robinson, is it really you?" she said. "I'm so glad! Who ever is this silly Other Bear who's been calling himself you?"

All the others began talking at once, saying, "Fancy

44

that," "The Other Bear took his name," "What a shame!" but Teddy Robinson and Jacqueline hardly heard them, they had so much to say to each other.

As for the Other Bear, he never said a word, but just sat up straight and proud, pretending not to notice, until the shop, man came in and fetched him away to be mended.

After that it was Teddy Robinson's turn. When his arm had been fixed on again the man pinned a label on him and carried him into the shop. There on the counter sat the Other Bear, also with a label on, all ready to go home.

The man put them down side by side, but the two teddy bears took no notice of each other. Each of them was trying hard to read the other one's label without looking. Then all of a sudden they both looked very surprised indeed.

"I say!" said Teddy Robinson, "is that your label?"

"Yes," said the Other Bear. "Is that yours?" For both the labels had Teddy Robinson written on them.

"I say, I'm awfully sorry," said Teddy Robinson.

" I say! Is that your label?"

"I'd no idea there was anyone else in the world with the same name as me. You must have had rather a horrid time in there with every one thinking you were pretending to be me. No wonder you were so quiet."

"Least said soonest mended," said the Other Bear, "and I *was* soonest mended."

"So you were," said Teddy Robinson. "But I am sorry."

"I thought you were making it up," said the Other Bear. "After all, Robinson is such a distinguished name. I'm surprised at *you* having it."

They were still both busy being surprised when the shop man came back, carrying a big telephone book.

"They asked me to phone when this one was ready," he said to his wife, "and now I've gone and lost their number." He turned over the pages. "Hmmm," he said, "just as I thought, pages and pages of Robinsons. Why, there must be more than a thousand of them. I'll never find the right one."

He went away again, scratching his head.

"Pages and pages of Robinsons?" said Teddy Robinson. "Well, bless my braces!"

"*And*," said the Other Bear solemnly, "if even half of those Robinsons have teddy bears it means there must be about four-hundred-and-ninety-nine other Teddy Robinsons, besides me."

"What about me?" said Teddy Robinson.

"You're just one of the four-hundred-and-ninety-nine other ones," said the Other Bear.

"Well, blow me up and stick me down, I think I'll change my name to Brown," said Teddy Robinson.

But at that minute the shop door opened and in came Deborah and Mummy. Teddy Robinson forgot all about changing his name to Brown, and all about all the other Teddy Robinsons, he was so pleased to see them.

Deborah hugged him and admired his mended arm.

"How does it feel to have two again?" she asked.

"Fine," said Teddy Robinson, swivelling it round as fast as it would go. "I got so used to having only one that it felt like having two, so now I've got two it feels more like three. I only need one more and I shall feel like a windmill."

Just then Deborah saw the Other Bear on the counter.

"*Look*, Mummy!" she said. "It's another Teddy Robinson."

"Why, so it is!" said Mummy.

"How funny that such an ordinary-looking bear should have our name," said Deborah.

"Well, ours is a very ordinary name," said Mummy, laughing. "There must be hundreds of

Teddy Robinsons, when you come to think of it."

"But only one really Special one like mine," said Deborah, hugging him all over again.

And that is the end of the story about how Teddy Robinson went to the Dolls' Hospital.

4

Teddy Robinson and
the China Gnome

One day Teddy Robinson and Deborah were looking at the marigolds and radishes coming up in their garden when the postman came by with a big parcel for Deborah. On one side it had a label which said FRAGILE, HANDLE WITH CARE.

"Now, what can that be?" said Deborah, and she ran indoors with it and sat Teddy Robinson down on the table so that he could watch while she opened it.

"Fragile. Handle with care," said Deborah. "I wonder what it is."

"It's got a beautiful name," said Teddy Robinson. "I wish my name was Fragile, but of course I haven't got a handle."

"No, it isn't a name," said Deborah, "and it doesn't mean it's got a handle. It means it's precious and mustn't be dropped or kicked around in case it gets broken."

"Ah," said Teddy Robinson, and he began singing:

"Fragile, fragile
Teddy R.,
what a precious bear I are.
Never leave me on the ground
in case I'm squashed or kicked around.
Fragile, fragile——"

"Don't be silly," said Deborah, "you aren't fragile. I expect this is some kind of ornament, that's what."

"Well, I shall be called Fragile too," said Teddy Robinson. "I shall have it for my second name."

Deborah pulled off the brown paper and opened the box, and there inside, among a lot of straw shavings, she found a china gnome sitting on a china toadstool. He had a bright blue jacket, a pointed red hat, and a long white beard.

"Oh, how sweet!" she said. "I believe it's an ornament. And there's a letter here too, it says 'love

from Uncle Michael.' I must go and show Mummy."
And off she ran.

"An Ornament," said Teddy Robinson to himself several times over. "An Ornament. It sounds rather an important thing to be. More important than Bear or Cat or Dog," and he began wondering what it was that made an ornament an Ornament, and not just something ordinary.

Deborah came running back.

"Yes," she said, "it *is* an ornament. Aren't I lucky? I've had lots of toys, but I've never had an ornament of my own before. I shall keep it here always," and she put it on the end of the mantelpiece, next to Daddy's pipe-rack.

"But that's where I sit," said Teddy Robinson.

"Only sometimes," said Deborah. "You can sit anywhere because you're a teddy bear. Ornaments have to go on the mantelpiece because they're fragile."

"Well, that settles it," said Teddy Robinson. "I'll be Fragile too. If he sits in my place, then I'll sit in his box. Do you mind lifting me in, very carefully?"

Teddy Fragile Robinson.

So Deborah lifted him into the box, and Teddy Robinson sat among the straw shavings and felt very precious indeed.

He began singing a little song about it:

"Fragile is my middle name,
handle me with care,
Teddy Fragile Robinson,
the ornamental bear."

53

But just then Mummy called to Deborah to bring the box out into the kitchen, because she didn't want the straw shavings all over the carpet. So Teddy Robinson was lifted out again, and that was the last he saw of the box.

He sat on the table and looked up at the china gnome. It wasn't a very friendly looking ornament, but he thought he had better be polite, so he said, "I hope you're comfortable up there? You get a nice view of everything, being so high up, don't you? I often sit there myself."

The china gnome didn't even turn his head, but said in a cracked and crusty voice, "I'm surprised they let you sit up here. The mantelpiece is the place for ornaments, not for toys. I am a very precious and fragile ornament."

"Well, I'm not exactly a toy," said Teddy Robinson. "I am a very precious and fragile teddy bear. I don't wind up or run about on wheels, so you wouldn't exactly call me a toy."

"Oh, yes, I would," said the china gnome. "A soft toy, that's what you are, and you ought to be kept in the toy-cupboard. That's the place for soft toys."

"*Nothing*," said Teddy Robinson loudly.

"What do you mean?"

"What I say. Deborah's always told me that if I can't think of a polite answer it's better to say nothing. So that's what I said."

After that he was quiet for a long while because he was thinking all over again about what it was that made an ornament an Ornament, and not just something ordinary.

"Why are you staring at me like that?" said the china gnome.

"I was wondering what it is you've got that I haven't," said Teddy Robinson.

"You haven't got a beard, or a pointed hat."

"No, you're right. I wonder I didn't think of it."

When Deborah came back again Teddy Robinson said, "Would you be so kind as to make me a pointed hat?"

"Yes, if you like," said Deborah, and she made him one out of newspaper.

"And now would you get some cotton wool and some string?"

"What ever for?" said Deborah.

"To make me a beard," said Teddy Robinson.

So Deborah fetched them, and she did just as Teddy Robinson told her, and put a big lump of cotton wool over the lower part of his face, and tied it round his head with a piece of string.

"Now put me on the mantelpiece," he said, "and tell me how many ornaments you see there."

Deborah stood back and looked at the mantelpiece.

"I see the clock," she said, "and Daddy's pipe-rack, and one china ornament, and my dear old teddy bear, with cotton wool all over his face and a paper hat on."

"Oh," said Teddy Robinson, "you're quite sure I don't look like an ornament?"

"Quite sure," said Deborah, laughing. "You look rather funny, really."

"All right," said Teddy Robinson. "Take them off again. There's no point in making a fool

"You're quite sure I don't look like an ornament?"

of myself for nothing."

Deborah had just taken them off again when there was a ring at the doorbell, and a moment later in came Andrew. He admired the china gnome very much, and Deborah told him all about how it had come when she and Teddy Robinson were in the garden.

"And that reminds me," she said, "my radishes are nearly ready to be picked. Come and see."

"I'll just fetch Spotty in," said Andrew, "I left him in the hall."

Spotty was Andrew's toy dog who usually came

with him when he came to play with Deborah. Teddy Robinson didn't care for him much because he always wanted to argue, so he quickly put on his Thinking Face and pretended to be making up poetry.

Andrew put them side by side in the arm-chair.

"They can talk to each other while we're busy," he said.

When the others had gone the spotted dog stared hard at the gnome with his black boot-button eyes, and said rudely, "That's new. What is it?"

"It's an ornament," whispered Teddy Robinson.

"Ah, yes, of course. Very useful things, ornaments," said the spotted dog, who always knew everything.

"What for?" asked Teddy Robinson.

"For being ornamental, of course," said Spotty.

"Oh," said Teddy Robinson. "Yes, of course. What does ornamental mean, exactly?"

"It's what ornaments are," said Spotty. "Surely you knew that?"

"Yes," said Teddy Robinson. "Of course. I don't know why I asked."

"Nor do I," said Spotty. He then stared hard at the china gnome again and barked rudely, "Hey, Mister Ornament! How do you like living with a teddy bear who doesn't know what ornamental means?"

The china gnome said, in a sharp, cracked voice, "I don't like it at all. Neither do I like being shouted at by a rude dog who ought to be outside in a kennel."

The spotted dog looked very surprised.

"This place seems more like a zoo than a house," said the china gnome. "You ought to be outside in the garden."

"Oh, no," said Teddy Robinson, "Spotty isn't a real dog, he's a real *toy* dog; same as I'm not a real bear, but a real *teddy* bear."

"Then he ought to go in the toy cupboard too," said the gnome.

There was a rustling noise at the open window, and the Next Door Kitten jumped up on the sill.

"Hallo," she purred, when she saw Teddy Robinson in the chair. "Are you coming out?"

"Not just now," said Teddy Robinson, "but won't you come in?"

"Thank you," said the Next Door Kitten, and she jumped through the window and landed on the arm of the chair.

"Who's the old gentleman on the mantelpiece?" she whispered through her whiskers.

"*That*," said the spotted dog in a loud, rude voice, "is the ugliest, nastiest——"

But Teddy Robinson said quickly, "Sssh! He's an ornament. He's come to live here."

The Next Door Kitten jumped lightly on to the mantelpiece and picked her way carefully along to the china gnome.

"Miaou do you do?" she said politely. "What purrrfectly lovely weather we're having."

"Get down! Get down at once!" snapped the china gnome. "How dare you get up here?"

The Next Door Kitten stepped back, surprised.

"But I often come up here," she said. "I come to talk to Teddy Robinson when he's sitting up here."

"Well, he's not going to sit up here any longer,"

said the gnome. "I don't like my sitting-room cluttered up with a lot of soft toys. I'm going to arrange for him to live in the toy cupboard. It isn't as if he were an ornament. As for you, get down at once and go back in the garden where you belong. I won't have wild animals in my room."

"But it's not your room," said the Next Door Kitten, "it's Teddy Robinson's, and he invited me in."

"Yes, I did!" shouted Teddy Robinson from the arm-chair, "but I never invited you. You just came in

"You just came in a parcel without being asked."

a parcel without being asked. I've tried to be polite to you and make you feel at home. I've let you sit in my place on the mantelpiece, but all you've done is be rude to me and my friends, so now I'm not going to try to make you feel at home any more. A gnome in the home is a terrible bore, and I don't want a gnome in my home any more. I shall ask Deborah to have you taken away."

He stopped for breath; then he said, "If I wasn't so angry I'd make a song about it. I nearly did by mistake."

Just then they heard footsteps outside. The Next Door Kitten turned quickly, brushing against the china gnome by mistake, and jumped down off the mantelpiece. At the same minute the china gnome fell with a thud on to the carpet.

No one spoke. The Next Door Kitten jumped out of the window, and sat washing her paws quietly on the ledge outside, as if nothing had happened. Then Teddy Robinson peered over the edge of the chair to see what had happened to the china gnome. He was still all in one piece, but there was a long crack down one side of his blue china jacket.

"Poor thing," said Teddy Robinson kindly, "I'm afraid you're cracked."

"Mind your own business," said the china gnome, and his voice sounded crustier and more cracked than ever. "I don't talk to soft toys."

"Well, I may be soft," said Teddy Robinson, "but I'm glad I'm not cracked."

Then the door opened and in came Deborah and Andrew.

"Oh!" said Deborah, "my ornament has fallen down!"

"And it's cracked down one side," said Andrew.

"Never mind," said Mummy, coming in after them, "it won't show when he's in the garden where he belongs."

"In the garden?" said Deborah, surprised.

"Yes," said Mummy, "he's a garden ornament. Didn't you read Uncle Michael's letter?"

"Oh, no, I forgot!" said Deborah. "It was such grown-up writing. But I thought he'd sit on the mantelpiece."

"Oh, no," said Mummy, "I don't think he'd look

right in here at all, but he'll be lovely in your garden."

"Oh, yes! He can look after the plants!" said Deborah.

"And frighten the birds away," said Teddy Robinson.

"Like a scarecrow," said the spotted dog.

So the china gnome was taken out and put in Deborah's garden, all among the radishes and marigolds, where he really looked quite pretty. Then Deborah found Uncle Michael's letter and read it aloud to Teddy Robinson. It said:

DEAR DEBORAH,

I hope you will like this little gnome for your garden. I think his name must be Grumpy because he looks rather cross, so he may be useful for frightening the slugs and earwigs away. I didn't buy you an indoor ornament because of course you have always got Teddy Robinson.

Love from,

UNCLE MICHAEL

"I think that is a very sensible letter," said Teddy Robinson. "I always did like Uncle Michael. Can I sit on the mantelpiece again now?"

"Of course," said Deborah, and she lifted him up.

"There's just one thing more I want to know," said Teddy Robinson. "What exactly is an ornament?"

"Why, you funny old boy," said Deborah. "Surely you knew that? It's something you put on a shelf because it looks pretty."

"Well, fancy that!" said Teddy Robinson. "Then I've been an Ornament all along and I never knew."

And that is the end of the story about
Teddy Robinson and the china gnome.

5

Teddy Robinson
Goes Up a Tree

One day Deborah said to Teddy Robinson, "Mary Anne is coming to play to-day, and she's bringing Jacqueline."

"Hooray," said Teddy Robinson. Jacqueline was his favourite of all the dolls he knew, and he hadn't seen her since they had been in the Dolls' Hospital together.

"Have her eyes been mended?" he asked.

"Yes," said Deborah, "and Mary Anne says she is looking more beautiful than ever."

"What colour are they?" asked Teddy Robinson.

"I forgot to ask," said Deborah. "Blue, I expect. I like blue."

"Or pink," said Teddy Robinson. "I like pink, and they would match her dress."

And he looked forward to seeing Jacqueline, with her eyes open at last, in the beautiful pink silk dress and bonnet that she always wore.

While Deborah ran down to the shops to buy some Dolly Mixture for them all to share, Teddy Robinson sat in the garden and thought about what he might be doing when Jacqueline arrived.

"It would be nice," he said to himself, "if she should just happen to come along when I just happened to be doing something that just *happened* to be rather clever or special or grown-up. Not on purpose, of course, but just if it happened to happen that way."

And he began wondering whether he might perhaps be swinging from a tree by only one arm, or riding Deborah's tricycle without his paws on the handlebars, or striding up and down the garden in his Wellington boots, pushing a wheelbarrow, like the gardener.

But I can't swing from a tree even with two arms, he thought, and I can't ride a tricycle, and I haven't got any Wellington boots, so none of those things will do. I must think again.

He had just decided that perhaps it would be best if he was found reading a grown-up book

riding Deborah's tricycle

without his paws on the handlebars

(without any pictures) and humming a little tune to himself (to show it was quite easy) when Timmy White came into the garden.

Timmy White belonged to Mrs White, the lady who sometimes came to help with the cleaning, and he had come out into the garden hoping to find Deborah. But Deborah was still out, and as Timmy White was a very shooty, shouty, bang-bang-bang sort of boy, Teddy Robinson thought it better just

or striding up and down the garden in his wellington boots, pushing a wheelbarrow

to stay quiet and hope he wouldn't be noticed.

Timmy White ran up and down the lawn, making fierce machine-gun noises with his mouth, and shooting at people who weren't there till they were all dead. Then he picked up a ball and threw it so far that it went right over the wall. After that he galloped all the way round the garden, picking things up and throwing them down again, until he came to where Teddy Robinson was sitting. Then

69

all of a sudden, before he had time to say a word, Timmy White had picked him up and thrown him high into the air.

Up and up went Teddy Robinson, higher and higher, and then—swish!—he fell right into the middle of the apple-tree. A sea of green leaves brushed his face as he began falling again, and then suddenly he stopped with a jerk and found himself sitting astride a branch.

When he was quite sure he had stopped falling Teddy Robinson looked down through the leaves and saw that he was still a long way up from the garden. In the distance he could see Timmy White running away into the house.

"Well, I never," said Teddy Robinson. "Fancy him doing that. And fancy me finding myself here. I seem to have happened on to this branch without quite knowing how. What you might call an Oblivious Coincidence."

"Goodness, what a shock you gave me!" chirped a bird, peering down from above with frightened eyes. "I'm all of a flutter."

"I do beg your pardon," said Teddy Robinson; "but I've just been the Victim of an Oblivious Coincidence."

"What does that mean?" said the bird.

"I don't know," said Teddy Robinson. "I've just made it up, but they're jolly long words, aren't they, and I've just come a jolly long way up. I've never been as high as this in my life before."

"I'm higher than you," said the bird.

"I dare say you are," said Teddy Robinson, "but you don't have to get down again. I do."

"Shall I push you with my beak?" said the bird, flapping its wings.

"Oh, no, don't do that!" said Teddy Robinson, and his voice went up into a squeak. "Do stop flapping. You make me feel all wobbly. Just tell me what you would do if you were me —there's a good bird."

"But that's just what I should do," said the bird. "I should flap my wings to stop myself falling."

"But I haven't any," squeaked Teddy Robinson.

The bird flew down a little way and looked at

Teddy Robinson's furry arms carefully.

"Try flapping those," he said. "They'd probably do as well."

"But I seem to need them for holding on with."

"Well, you can't have it both ways," said the bird. "You can't expect to hold on and fly at the same time."

"No, I suppose I can't," said Teddy Robinson. "Perhaps I'll just hold on for now, and think about flying later."

The bird flew down beside him and began hopping up and down on the branch.

"Bounce a bit," he said. "It's quite fun, especially when the wind's blowing like it is now."

"Ooo-err, look out!" said Teddy Robinson, as the branch waved up and down under him.

But it was all right. He seemed to be stuck quite firmly where he was, and after a while he stopped feeling wobbly, and began to enjoy himself instead.

"This is very jolly," he said, bouncing a little higher. "I've never been so high up in the world before. I should think I'm jolly nearly at the top of the tree. It's making me feel quite bouncy. I always knew I was a clever bear, but I'd no idea I was as clever as this, to be sitting right up here all by myself. Why, anybody'd think I'd climbed up here just for fun. What a very clever bear I are! It really is very jolly getting above myself like this." And he began singing:

"Three cheers for me
at the top of the tree,
the cleverest bear you ever did see.
Nobody knows
how clever I are
Who would suppose
I could climb so far?
Three cheers for me
at the top of the tree.
Oh, what a wonderful bear I be!"

Just then he heard voices, and, peeping down, Teddy Robinson saw Deborah searching about at the foot of the tree.

"*Three cheers for me at the top of the tree.*"

"That's funny," she was saying. "Where's Teddy Robinson? I'm sure I left him here. He was waiting to see you. He couldn't have walked off all by himself."

"Goodness, they must have come already!" said Teddy Robinson. And then he suddenly remembered this was just what he'd wanted. To be found doing something rather clever and grown-up as if it was the easiest thing in the world. So he stared up into the branches, and said in rather a loud voice, "What a wonderful view one gets from up here!" Then he bounced gently up and down again in the wind, and began singing to himself in an airy sort of way:

"Easy-peasy, pudding and pie,
easy as pie
to climb so high.
The view from here
at the top of the tree
is just the thing
for a chap like me.
Easy as pie,
why don't you try?
Easy-peasy, pudding and pie."

There was silence for a moment. Teddy Robinson peeped down with one eye and saw Deborah staring up at him through the leaves as if she could hardly believe her eyes.

"Easy as pie," he said again.

"Teddy Robinson!" said Deborah. "What ever

75

are you doing up there?"

"Oh, just looking around," said Teddy Robinson, in a light, careless sort of voice. "Have our visitors arrived?"

"Yes," said Deborah, "but what have you been *doing?*"

"Doing? Well, I've been bird-watching, as a matter of fact."

"*Bird-watching?* But how did you get up there?"

"How did I get up here? Oh. I—er—I just happened to be thinking about something, and then before I knew where I was I happened to find myself here. Just like that."

Deborah looked as if she didn't believe it, so Teddy Robinson went on, "You know how easy it is, if you're thinking about something else, to fall down by mistake. Well, if you happen to be thinking about something rather important, as I was, I suppose you might just happen to fall up instead of down, mightn't you?"

Deborah didn't say anything, she was still so surprised.

"—if you forgot to notice which way you were going, I mean," said Teddy Robinson.

But Deborah wasn't listening any more.

"Oh, dear, oh, dear!" she was saying. "How shall we get him down?"

"Ask your mummy; perhaps she's got a ladder," said Mary Anne.

"Oh, yes," said Deborah, and they ran off into the house, leaving Jacqueline on the rug at the foot of the tree.

"Oh, Teddy Robinson!" said Jacqueline, gazing up to where she could just see the ends of his legs, "I never dreamt I should find you doing anything quite so wonderful as climbing a tree. What a very clever bear you are!"

Teddy Robinson was just going to say, "Yes, aren't I?" but he remembered in time, and said instead, "Oh, it's nothing really. It passes the time and makes a change."

"I do hope they'll be able to get you down soon," said Jacqueline. "Did you know my eyes were mended?"

"Yes, I am glad," said Teddy Robinson. "I've been looking forward to seeing you with them open."

"And I've been looking forward to seeing *you* with them open," said Jacqueline. "It will be the first time."

Teddy Robinson suddenly went very quiet up in the tree. He had forgotten that Jacqueline would now be able to see him. He looked down at his short, fat legs with their worn brown fur and his shabby trousers, and began thinking very hard, trying to remember what he had told her about himself.

"Er—Jacqueline, did I ever tell you how big I was?"

"Oh, yes, Teddy Robinson, lots of times!"

"Oh!"

He thought for another minute; then he said, "And how big, exactly, was that?"

Jacqueline laughed. "What a funny question!" she said. "As big as you are, of course."

"Perhaps I'm not quite so big as you thought I meant I was," said Teddy Robinson. "I mean

I might look smaller now."

"Of course you won't," said Jacqueline. "Why should you? Teddy bears don't shrink."

"No," said Teddy Robinson, "but the funny thing is I am beginning to feel rather small. It's come on quite suddenly. I feel as if I'm getting smaller and smaller every minute."

He was quiet for a little while, then he called down again. "Jacqueline, what sort of colour did I tell you my fur was?"

"Didn't you say it was a soft golden brown?"

"Did I?" said Teddy Robinson unhappily. "Oh, dear, I hope I didn't, because now I come to think of it I don't think it is a very golden brown. I think it's more what you'd call a sort of brownish brown. And there isn't a lot of it."

Jacqueline laughed again. "You are a funny bear, Teddy Robinson. Why should you want to make yourself sound so plain and ordinary, when I know you're not?"

"Well, it's just come to me that perhaps I am rather plain and ordinary after all," said Teddy

Robinson. "Much plainer and ordinarier than I thought I was a little while ago."

"I don't believe you," said Jacqueline.

"But you must believe me!" said Teddy Robinson. "Listen, I can hear them coming. Please let me tell you quickly what I'm really like," and he began gabbling very fast. "I'm a plain and ordinary family bear, not very dark and not very fair, a brownish brown, with brownish eyes, and only a *middling* kind of size. My ear came off a while ago, it's mended now but the stitches show, my fur's worn thin with too much kissing, one of my braces' buttons is missing, and—"

But before he could say any more the others had come back. Mummy was with them, carrying a long stick with a feather duster on top of it. She poked about among the branches saying, "That naughty Timmy White must have thrown him up here. Ah, here he is!" and a moment later Teddy Robinson went tumbling through the leaves to the ground.

Deborah picked him up and brushed the twigs off him, and Mummy said, "Well, he doesn't seem any the worse for his adventure," and went back to the house. Then he was put to sit on the rug beside Jacqueline while Deborah and Mary Anne shared out the Dolly Mixture on to dolls' plates.

Teddy Robinson stared hard at the worn brown fur on his short, fat legs and felt smaller than ever.

— felt smaller than ever.

It seemed such a silly sort of come-down for some one who'd been at the top of a tree, to be poked down on the end of a feather duster.

But when at last he looked up he saw that Jacqueline was smiling at him, and her eyes were big and blue and shining.

"Oh, Teddy Robinson," she said, "you look just how I've always imagined you! I knew you were big and brave and handsome, but I did hope you didn't look proud. And you don't. I'm so glad. I think it's so important that brave and splendid people should look kind and cosy as well, don't you?"

And that is the end of the story about how
Teddy Robinson went up a tree.

6

Teddy Robinson
Goes to the Fair

One day Teddy Robinson sat on the window-sill of Deborah's room and thought about all the things he most specially wanted. Deborah was helping Mummy to bake a gingerbread man that morning, so he had a nice long time to think.

First he thought how jolly it would be if a fairy came by and asked him to go to tea with the Man in the Moon. But that was only pretend thinking, and he knew it couldn't really happen, so he decided to think about real things instead. He found there were quite a lot of real things he wanted.

I would like to be able to play the piano, he thought, then I could make the music for the songs I think of; and he had a picture in his mind of how nice he would look sitting up at the piano on a high stool, while everybody sat round listening to him playing.

He had a picture in his mind of how nice he would look sitting up at the piano

Then I want a satchel, he thought, and a pair of Wellington boots, and I would like to ride on a horse; but, more than all the other things, what I *most* specially want is to drive a motor-car.

He had often been for rides on buses with Deborah, and when they had been lucky enough to have the front seat on top he had done quite a lot of things to help the driver make the bus start and stop. He had found that when the traffic lights were changing from red to yellow he had only to push forward once or twice and the bus would start. And when the traffic lights were changing from green back to yellow and red all he had to do was to sit back sharply and the bus would stop.

But, of course, that was not the same as really driving. It was only helping.

"I must practise driving a motor-car all by myself," he said, "just in case I ever have the chance."

So he sat on the window-sill and rocked gently from side to side, growling to make a motor-car noise. Then he held the middle button of his jacket between his paws and turned it round, first this way and then that, to practise going round corners. He had just decided that he was now good enough at driving to take himself for a long pretend ride before dinner, when Deborah came running into the room.

"Guess what, Teddy Robinson!" she said. "The fair has come, and we're going this afternoon!"

"Good," said Teddy Robinson. "In that case I won't go for a pretend ride after all. What is a fair?"

"Oh, it's lovely," said Deborah. "There are swings

To practise going round corners

and roundabouts and all sorts of things. You shall come for a ride with me."

"What on?" asked Teddy Robinson.

"On a horse on the roundabout," said Deborah.

"Oh, *very* nice," said Teddy Robinson. "That's one of the things I was specially wanting."

While Deborah brushed his fur with the dolls' brush, and put on his best purple dress that he always wore for parties, Teddy Robinson began to sing to himself because he was so happy:

"The fair, the fair,
we're off to the fair.
What shall we do when we get there?
Ride, of course,
on a galloping horse;
a nice little girl and a Big Brown Bear."

"Don't be silly," said Deborah. "It ought to be a big girl and a middling-sized bear."

"It sounded better the other way," said Teddy Robinson, "and anyway I always feel big when I'm happy."

After dinner they all set off.

Mummy had given Deborah two shillings to spend at the fair, and she and Teddy Robinson were busy all the way there thinking how they were going to spend it.

"It will make four rides if they are sixpence each," said Mummy.

"Or three rides and one candy floss," said Deborah.

"Or four candy flosses?" said Teddy Robinson.

"Yes, but they're so big we shan't want four," said Deborah.

"Shan't we?" said Teddy Robinson. "What are they?"

"They're great big fluffy things on sticks," said Deborah. "They look like pink cotton wool, but you can eat them."

Soon they heard the noise of the fair music, and a moment later they turned the corner and were in the fairground.

Teddy Robinson thought he had never seen anything so exciting. There were so many things to look at that he didn't know which to look at first. But Deborah decided for him.

"Look, Teddy Robinson," she said. "There's the roundabout with the horses. Shall we go on that first?"

"Oh, yes," he said.

So they waited for the roundabout to stop and then ran to choose their horse. It was a beautiful roundabout, all painted in red and gold, and each of the horses had its own name painted on its side.

"Can I have a horse to myself?" asked Teddy Robinson.

"No, you might fall off," said Deborah, "and anyway we'd have to pay extra."

So they chose a grey and white spotted horse called Nellie, and climbed up on to her back together. Teddy Robinson sat in front with his paws round Nellie's neck. "Don't hold me, then," he said.

"All right," said Deborah. Then the music began and off they went. Mummy stood and watched

The music began and off they went

them as they went round and round, and sometimes she waved as they went by. Teddy Robinson didn't dare wave back in case he fell off, and as they went faster and faster he was glad to feel that Deborah was holding him after all. It was most exciting. He began to sing his little fair song again, but this time he changed it to

"Gee up, Nellie, to the fair,
  round and round till we get there;
  gallop along as fast as you dare
  with the nice little girl and the Big
      Brown Bear."

When the music stopped and the horses stood still again they felt they couldn't bear to get down just yet, so they stayed on Nellie for another ride. Deborah gave the man another sixpence and off they went again.

It was just as lovely as the first ride, but it seemed even shorter. Next time the horses stopped they said good-bye to Nellie and climbed down.

"Thank you," said Teddy Robinson. "That was very nice."

After that they went to the candy-floss stall. They gave the lady sixpence, and she made them a candy floss that was nearly as big as Teddy Robinson.

"Good gracious!" he said. "Shall we be able to eat it all to-day?"

"Shall we be able to eat it all today?"

91

But though it looked so big it was very fluffy, and it didn't take them long to eat their way right through it.

"We've only got sixpence left already," said Deborah when they had finished. "We'd better go and look at some other things before we decide what to spend it on."

They stopped at a stall where some people were throwing darts at a board.

"What are they doing that for?" asked Deborah.

"If they get a big enough number they win a prize," said Mummy.

Deborah and Teddy Robinson decided they would save their last sixpence for something else, but they stayed for a while to watch.

At the back of the stall were the prizes. There were a lot of tea-sets and glass dishes and some baskets of fruit, and standing up in the middle were five very large pale blue teddy bears. They were wrapped in "Cellophane" and looked beautifully new and shiny, but they had rather silly faces.

Teddy Robinson looked at them for a long time.

Then he looked down at his own light brown fur which wasn't shiny any more. He began to feel rather small, and although he was wearing his best purple dress he suddenly felt old and shabby. He looked at Deborah out of the corner of his eye and saw that she too was staring at the teddy bears. He wondered if she thought they were beautiful, and hoped she didn't.

He began to feel rather small

"I think it's rather soppy to be pale blue, don't you?" he said.

"Yes," said Deborah. "I'd rather have your colour to live with. Those teddy bears have to look specially beautiful, poor things."

"Why are they poor things?" asked Teddy Robinson.

"Because they are prizes waiting to be won," said Deborah. "You wouldn't like to be a prize, would you?"

"Oh, no," said Teddy Robinson, and he began to feel sorry for the big pale blue teddy bears, and hoped they hadn't heard him say it was soppy to be that colour.

After they had looked at quite a few other things they decided to spend their last sixpence on another kind of roundabout. This was one where they sat in a little chair with their feet sticking out in front of them; and as they went round and round they seemed to go higher and higher. They both thought it was rather like being in an aeroplane.

"That was nice, wasn't it?" said Deborah, when they got down again. "I hope you enjoyed it."

"Oh, yes, I hope I did," said Teddy Robinson,

"because it was my last ride. But I think I liked Nellie better."

"So did I," said Deborah.

And then, just as they were going on their way out, they saw a roundabout with motor-cars and motorbikes which they hadn't seen before. They stopped to look at it, and Teddy Robinson felt rather sad.

"I never specially wanted to go in an aeroplane chair," he said, "but I did want to ride in a motor-car."

"I haven't any money left for a ride in one of those," said Deborah.

"I know," said Teddy Robinson, "but let's just look at them. Let's choose which one we would ride in if we did have enough money."

So they walked all the way round, looking at each of the cars in turn, and they both decided that a bright blue one was the nicest.

"If I sat in the front seat," said Teddy Robinson, "do you think my paws would reach the driving-wheel?"

"I think they might," said Deborah.

"Couldn't I just try?" he asked. "Just for a minute?"

"No, I don't think so," said Deborah. "Don't worry me, there's a good boy."

"Oh, no," said Teddy Robinson, "I won't worry you. I'll think about it instead." And he began thinking to himself in a round-and-round sort of way, like this, "If I could sit *in* it, for only a minute, sit *in* it, a minute, before they begin it, if I could sit *in* it . . ."

"Oh, all right, then," said Deborah, "just for a minute. I don't expect the man will mind"; and she lifted Teddy Robinson up and sat him in the front seat of the little blue car.

"Oh, look!" she said. "Your paws *do* reach the driving-wheel."

"So they do!" said Teddy Robinson, and he felt very pleased.

Deborah was so busy admiring him that she never noticed that the roundabout was just going to start. She turned round to show Mummy, and at that minute the cars began to move slowly round.

Before she had time to lift him off again Teddy Robinson was out of reach, going round and round in the little blue car all by himself.

He sat up very straight with his paws on the driving-wheel and felt bigger and better than he had ever felt before. As he went round and round, faster and faster, the wind ruffled his fur and he felt as if he was going for miles and miles all by himself.

The wind ruffled his fur

Every now and again he saw Deborah, and each time he passed her she waved her hand at him. He didn't wave back because he didn't want to take his paw off the driving-wheel. It was so lovely to be really driving a motor-car at last, and all by himself too. He began to feel a little song going round and round in his head as he went round and round on the roundabout:

> "Here I are, here I are,
> driving in a motor-car.
> What a clever bear I be.
> Don't forget to wave to me.
> Lucky, lucky Teddy R.,
> driving in a motor-car!"

And then at last the cars began to go slower and slower until they stopped. Deborah ran to lift him out.

"Oh, Teddy Robinson," she said, "I never meant you to have a ride, but wasn't it fun!"

"It was lovely," said Teddy Robinson, "and didn't I drive it well? I never bumped into any of the others."

After that it was time to go home. Teddy

Robinson felt so happy and pleased with himself that he even waved his paw to the pale blue bears as he passed their stall on the way out.

"I'm lucky not to be a prize at a fair," he said to himself. "In fact, I'm a jolly lucky chap altogether. I may not have learned to play the piano yet, and I still haven't got a satchel or a pair of Wellington boots, but I did ride on a horse, and I *have* driven a motor-car all by myself."

And that is the end of the story about how
Teddy Robinson went to the fair.

7

Teddy Robinson's Dreadful Accident

One day Teddy Robinson had a Dreadful Accident, and this is how it happened.

He and Deborah had decided to go for a little walk all by themselves; at least, Deborah was going to walk, and Teddy Robinson was going to be pushed in the dolls' pram.

"We will go by the pond," said Deborah, "and then you can watch the ducks."

"That will be nice," said Teddy Robinson. "Can I have a pillow behind me?"

"Yes," said Deborah, "you shall have the best dolls' pillow with the frill round it." And she tucked it in behind him, so that he could sit up straight all the way.

The pond where the ducks lived was not very far from home. They had only to go a little way up the road until they came to a steep path, and at the bottom of the path was the duck pond.

Deborah and Teddy Robinson had just reached the top of the steep little path when they met another little girl coming down the road. Her name was Mary Anne, and she too was pushing a dolls' pram.

Deborah said, "Hallo, Mary Anne," and Mary Anne said, "Hallo, Deborah," and they both started talking.

Teddy Robinson looked at the doll in the other pram, but he didn't say hallo to her, because she was lying down with her eyes shut. She was very beautiful, with a pink silk dress and a frilly bonnet to match, and she was covered with a satin eiderdown.

Deborah and Mary Anne talked to each other until Teddy Robinson was nearly growing tired of waiting; and then, just as they were saying good-bye at last, the Dreadful Accident happened.

A little wind blew up and lifted the eiderdown right off Mary Anne's beautiful doll, and sent it spinning away down the road. Deborah said, "Oh, look! Your eiderdown!" and ran to catch it. And

Teddy Robinson found that now Deborah had let go of the pram it was beginning to run downhill all by itself with him inside it.

Bumpety-bump it went, down the steep little path, faster and faster.

"Oh, my goodness!" said Teddy Robinson to

—down the steep little path, faster and faster—

himself. "I hope we shan't bump into that lamp-post at the bottom."

But that is just what they did. They went *crash* into the lamp-post, the pram turned sideways, and before you could say "Teddy Robinson" it had shot under the railings and gone *splash* into the pond.

Luckily for Teddy Robinson he fell out as the pram turned over, and a moment later he found himself lying in the mud at the edge of the pond. But the pram was upside down in the water with its wheels sticking up in the air, and the pillow was floating away.

"Goodness me!" said he. "What a lucky thing I fell out!"

In another moment he heard Deborah come rushing down the steep little hill, shouting, "Teddy Robinson! Where are you? Oh, where are you?" And then he saw her frightened face looking at him through the railings over his head.

"Oh, what are we to do?" she cried. "How ever shall I get you out? Are you drowned? Oh, what a dreadful accident!"

"No, I aren't drowned," said Teddy Robinson. "Don't cry. I'm quite all right really, but just run home and ask Mummy to come and get me out."

So Deborah ran off home as fast as she could, and Teddy Robinson lay in the mud and waited to be rescued.

Before long a duck came swimming over from the other side of the pond. As soon as it saw Teddy Robinson in the mud, and the pram upside down in the water, it said, "Quack!" in a very loud and surprised voice. Then it turned round and swam quickly back to tell the other ducks.

Teddy Robinson could hear them all quacking together over on the other side of the pond.

"Quack! Quack! He's flat on his back!"

"Who is? And where?"

"The bear, over there."

"Alas and alack! Who'll fetch him back?"

"Quick! Quick! Quack-quack-quack!"

And then they all came swimming over together and crowded round him, asking him questions, and making a great deal of noise to

They crowded round him.

show how worried they were.

Teddy Robinson told them what had happened.

"How awful!" they quacked. "What a dreadful thing! Fancy that! You'll never be the same again! Poor thing! Oh, quack-quack-quack!"

"I do feel rather wet and muddy," said Teddy Robinson, "but I don't think I'm as bad as all that."

"But you've grown so *thin*!" quacked one duck.

"And such a queer *colour*!" quacked another.

"And your *eyes* are so starey!" quacked a third.

"Have I really? Are they truly?" said Teddy Robinson, and he began to feel rather worried.

"If I could only sit up perhaps I could see my

105

reflection in the water," he said, "and then I should know how bad I am."

So the kind ducks pushed him gently with their bills until he was sitting upright, and Teddy Robinson looked down into the water. He couldn't see himself very clearly, because a little breeze was rippling over the top of the pond, but he was glad to see that he was all in one piece.

"I do look rather *trembly*," he said, "but I think it was only the shock. I had rather a fright, you know."

"Yes! Yes! A terrible fright!" quacked the ducks.

"I do look rather trembly."

"What a shock! What a shock! Quack! Quack!"

"But I think I'm all right now," said Teddy Robinson, "and somebody's coming to fetch me soon."

"Then, *we* must look after you until they come!" quacked the ducks, and they all crowded round him, quacking and fussing and trying to be helpful.

"Now, what would you like to eat?" they asked. "What about a little water weed? Not too much, but a nice little slimy piece?"

"Oh, no, thank you, I really couldn't," said Teddy Robinson.

"Well, then, you must have plenty of fresh air!" they quacked, and they all began flapping their wings up and down and fanning him.

"It's very kind of you," said Teddy Robinson, "but really I'm cold enough already."

"Then, we must keep you warm!" quacked the ducks, and they all sat on top of him, spreading out their feathers.

"I don't like to mention it," said Teddy Robinson,

"but your feet are awfully muddy, and I'm so muddy already it seems a pity to make it worse."

"Yes! Yes! So you are!" quacked the ducks. "Perhaps we had better wash you!" And they all began pushing him towards the water with their bills.

But at that minute Teddy Robinson heard the sound of voices coming down the path, so he was glad to be able to say, "Please don't bother! I can hear my people coming to fetch me. Thank you all very much indeed, but I shall be all right now. And, by the way, if any of you would like a little pillow you'll find one floating over there by the reeds."

"Oh, thank you!" quacked the ducks. "Just what we should like for our nests. Thank you! Good-bye! Quack! Quack!"

Then along came Deborah and Mummy, and Teddy Robinson was lifted up and passed through the railings, and the pram was lifted out of the water and turned the right way up.

Deborah carried Teddy Robinson home, holding

him carefully, because he was so wet and muddy, and looking at him with a worried face, because somehow he looked so different. Mummy wheeled the pram along behind.

"My poor boy!" said Deborah. "You look terribly thin, and your beautiful fur has all gone, and why are your eyes so round and surprised?"

"Because I had such a dreadful fright," said Teddy Robinson.

"No, it's only because he is wet," said Mummy. "We will wash him when we get home. And don't worry about his fur. I'm sure it will come up nice and fluffy when it's dry again, and then he will look like his old self."

"But I *did* have a fright," said Teddy Robinson. "She might be quite right, but I *did* have a fright."

"Yes, I'm sure you did," said Deborah.

So when they got home Teddy Robinson was given a bath in warm soapy water. Then Mummy spread a cloth on top of the cooker, where the plates were usually put to keep warm, and he sat up there to dry.

"Are you comfy?" asked Deborah.

But Teddy Robinson didn't feel like being comfy.

"I *did* have a fright," he kept saying. "I *did* have a fright. What a crash! What a smash! What a splish-splosh-splash!"

"Now, for goodness' sake stop talking about it," said Deborah. "It's all over now, so you must forget about it."

"But I don't want to forget about it yet," said Teddy Robinson. "It gives me a fright every time I think about it, so I want to go on talking about it until it stops frightening me; otherwise I might think about it by mistake some time, and it would give me a fright when I wasn't looking."

So he sat on top of the cooker and remembered it out loud four times over from beginning to end. Then he felt better.

"I think I'll come down now," he said.

"Are you dry?"

"Not quite, but I think it would be nice to sit in front of the fire with the dolls and tell them all about it. I feel as if I could enjoy it now. You haven't told them already, have you?"

"No," said Deborah. "I'll get them out of the toy-cupboard."

So out they all came, and they sat on the hearth-rug in a circle, and Teddy Robinson sat in the middle of them with his back to the fire, and felt very cosy and important.

"Oh, Teddy Robinson!" said all the dolls. "What has been happening to you? Why is your fur so spiky? Have you been swimming? Why are you sitting on a bath-towel?"

"Why is your fur so spiky?"

"I have been in a Dreadful Accident," said Teddy Robinson, "and I thought you might like to hear about it."

"Oh, yes! Tell us all about it, Teddy Robinson," said the dolls.

So Teddy Robinson said in a deep and important voice:

> "Behold the bear
> who had a big scare,
> who rolled in the pram
> from here to there——"

"What! *Our* pram?" asked the dolls.

"Yes," said Teddy Robinson. "Don't interrupt.

> "Behold the bear
> who went with a thud
> over the bank
> and into the mud——"

"What mud? Where?" asked the dolls.

"*Don't interrupt*," said Teddy Robinson, "and I'll tell you.

> "Rolled in the pram
> with a smash and a crash
> into the pond
> with a splish-splosh-splash——"

"Good gracious!" cried all the dolls. "Tell us about it from the beginning."

So Teddy Robinson told them the whole story, and the dolls listened right to the end without interrupting once more.

When he had finished they all said, "How brave you are, Teddy Robinson!"

"But didn't you *do* anything?" asked one of them. "Do you mean you just lay there and waited?"

"Sometimes that is the bravest thing you *can* do," said Teddy Robinson, "just stay where you are and wait to be found."

"Yes," said all the other dolls, "Teddy Robinson is quite right. How very brave he is!"

113

"And now," said Teddy Robinson, "I think it's time I was turned round. I seem to be nicely browned on that side."

So Deborah turned him round until his other side was quite dry too, then she brushed his fur with the dolls' hairbrush. It came up so beautifully soft and fluffy that it looked just like new. Deborah was quite excited.

"You *do* look lovely!" she cried. "Mummy said you would look like your old self again when your fur was dry; but it's even better than that—

"My fur has never looked so nice before"

you look like your *new* self!"

And she held him up in front of the mirror so that he could see himself.

"Oh, I do, don't I?" said Teddy Robinson. "I *am* glad I had that Dreadful Accident. It has made me feel quite special and important, and my fur has never looked so nice before."

"Not since it was new," said Deborah.

"No," he said, "and we wouldn't have noticed it so much then, because we didn't know each other so well, did we?"

And that is the end of the story about
Teddy Robinson's Dreadful Accident.

8

Teddy Robinson
and the Fairies

Once upon a time Teddy Robinson and Deborah went to stay for a few days with Auntie Sue in her cottage in the country.

They had a lovely time. All day long the bees buzzed in the garden and the cows mooed in the fields, and every evening Auntie Sue read them a fairy story out of a book that she used to enjoy when she was a little girl. So they went to sleep every night with their heads full of fairy stories and country things.

One afternoon Teddy Robinson said to Deborah, "I like it here. The flowers are full of honey, and the woods smell like hot blackberry jam. It's no wonder fairies choose to live in the country. Do you think we shall see any fairies while we are here?"

And Deborah said, "I don't know, Teddy Robinson; but you've just given me a good idea.

Let's go out now, all by ourselves, and see if we can find some!"

So they set off together down the lane.

Soon they came to a place where white flowers with long, twisted stalks were growing all over the hedge.

"I think a crown of those would suit me," said Deborah, and she pulled down a long string of the flowers and began to twist them into a garland to wear round her head.

"Yes," said Teddy Robinson. "I think they might suit me as well, don't you? Or should I look soppy?"

"No, they would suit you very well," said Deborah. "We shall look a bit more like fairies ourselves if we wear garlands of flowers. They all do in Auntie Sue's fairy book. Sit still and let me fit you."

So Teddy Robinson sat still and watched while Deborah made a garland for each of them, and fitted them on their heads. Then they set off down the lane again.

A little farther on they came to a turning where a narrow grassy path led off between trees and

Deborah made a garland for each of them.

bushes, and disappeared among the leaves. The trees met overhead like an archway, so that it all looked very green and quiet and secret.

"Oh, look!" said Deborah. "That is *just* the sort of place where fairies would live. It looks almost magic."

So very quietly they went down the little green lane, peeping here and peeping there, under leaves and into bushes, and up into the branches over their heads.

But not a sign of a fairy did they see.

"I'm sure if there *are* any fairies they would be here," said Deborah, after they had been looking for quite a long while. "I wonder why we can't find any."

... down the little green lane.

"Perhaps we are looking too hard," said Teddy Robinson. "Don't you think if we just sat down quietly and had a little rest they might come up to us and say hallo?"

"Of course not, silly boy," said Deborah. "Fairies have to be looked for, and I'm going on looking. You can sit down if you like." And she sat him down by the edge of the grassy path and went on a little way alone.

A moment later she came running back, very excited.

"Guess what, Teddy Robinson!" she called out. "I've found blackberries, lots and lots of them, and they're all ripe. I'm going to pick a whole bucketful for Auntie Sue."

"But have you got a whole bucket?" asked Teddy Robinson.

"No, I haven't got anything," said Deborah, "and my hands are full already. But I'll run back and get a basket. Will you be a good boy, Teddy Robinson, and sit here till I come back? Promise me not to move."

"Yes, I promise," said Teddy Robinson. "Just put my garland straight before you go, will you?"

So Deborah put his garland straight, then she kissed him good-bye, and ran off down the grassy path.

When she had gone it seemed very quiet in the

little green lane. There was no sound at all except the drowsy buzzing of flies, and not a leaf stirred in the green branches overhead. Teddy Robinson sat perfectly still and thought about how quiet it was, and how green it was; and after a while he began to make up a little song about it. It went like this:

"Quiet and green,
quiet and green,
bushes and treeses with grasses between.
Quiet and brown,
quiet and brown,
one teddy bear sitting quietly down;
quiet and brown
in the quiet and green,
all by himself—not a soul to be seen."

"Except me!" said a tiny voice, and Teddy Robinson saw that a beautiful furry caterpillar was crawling up his leg.

"Hallo!" he said. "That's a very fine fur coat you are wearing."

"Yes, isn't it?" said the caterpillar, and he wriggled round so that he could look down his own back and admire it.

"I have a fur coat too," said Teddy Robinson.

"Have you really?" said the caterpillar. "Where?"

"You're crawling over it now," said Teddy Robinson.

"Oh, am I?" said the caterpillar. "I'm so sorry. I'd no idea. You're so very large I quite thought this was a field I was walking in. I know I came up a very big hill just now."

"Yes, that was my leg," said Teddy Robinson.

"Dear me!" said the furry caterpillar. "Do forgive me. I wouldn't have walked on your fur coat for anything." And he hurried away to crawl down the other side.

"Don't mention it," said Teddy Robinson. "Please crawl about on me as much as you like. My fur is quite old, and I really don't mind."

But the caterpillar had gone scrambling down his other leg and was already hurrying away into the grass.

Teddy Robinson began humming to himself again:

"Quiet and green,
quiet and green,
bushes and treeses with grasses between . . ."

And then he stopped, because he felt almost sure that while he was humming he had heard other little voices singing different words to the same tune. But as soon as he was quiet everything else was quiet too.

"It must have been a think," said Teddy Robinson to himself. "I won't take any notice."

So he started again:

"Quiet and green,
quiet and green . . ."

Then he stopped suddenly and listened again. And this time he was quite sure, because the other little voices went on after he had stopped, and this is what they were singing:

"We haven't been seen,
we haven't been seen;
creep through the bushes and grasses between.
Better take care!
There's somebody there.
Mind where you step—it's a big brown bear."

Teddy Robinson held his breath and kept quite still. A moment later he heard a little rustling noise in the grasses behind him, and then a lot of tiny voices all began talking at once.

"It's all right," said one. "He isn't fierce."

"He's wearing flowers round his head," said another.

"Let's go and have a proper look at him," said a third.

There was a little more rustling and whispering behind Teddy Robinson, and then out they came. A whole crowd of fairies, not one of them half as big as himself, and all dressed in the prettiest colours he had ever seen, with tiny garlands of flowers round their heads. Teddy Robinson could hardly believe his eyes!

They flitted about in front of him. One or two of them spread their wings and flew a little way here and there. A beautiful little fairy with a star in her hair shook out the frills of her pink and yellow dress. Another, with a garland of forget-me-nots, threw a thistledown in the air and fanned it with her wings. And all the time, out of the corners of their eyes, they were watching Teddy Robinson and whispering about him to each other.

"Look," said one, who was dressed in a silver cobweb, "he is wearing a garland like ours. *I* think he might be a fairy person."

"He couldn't be," said another. "His feet are too big."

"And he isn't wearing a fairy dress," said a tiny one in rosy pink.

"He is extremely large," said all the fairies together, and then they all began talking at once again.

"He's bumpy and lumpy."

"His legs are stumpy."

"His back's too humpy."

"His face looks grumpy."

"It doesn't," said the cobweb fairy. "And look, he has lovely soft fur." And, reaching out a tiny hand, she stroked Teddy Robinson on the tummy. Then another fairy grew brave and came up to touch him, and then another, and another; and soon they were all pulling at his ears and poking him gently with their spiky little fingers.

Teddy Robinson felt a big laugh beginning to rumble inside of him.

all pulling at his ears and poking him gently

"Oh! You're tickling me!" he said.

At once all the fairies flew down, frightened, and stood looking at him from a little way off.

"He has a voice like a thunderstorm," they said. "Perhaps he is a new kind of giant."

Teddy Robinson was pleased at this, but he didn't want to frighten them away, so he said, "No, I am not a giant."

"What are you, then?" they asked.

"I'm a bear."

"A human bear?"

"No, just a teddy bear."

"Fancy that! Can you fly?"

"No," said Teddy Robinson. "I wish I could, but bears don't have wings."

"Do you wish you were a fairy like us?"

"I don't know," said Teddy Robinson. "I quite like being a teddy bear really, but I should *love* to fly. I've always wanted to fly."

"Come with us to Fairyland, then," said the fairies. "Come and live with us, and we will make you a pair of wings."

"I couldn't come and *live* with you," said Teddy Robinson, "because I live with Deborah. But I should love to come for a visit."

"Oh, no!" said all the fairies. "That would never do. If you come with us you must stay for always. Nobody is allowed to come back once they know all the fairy secrets."

"Then, I'm afraid I can't come," said Teddy Robinson sadly. "You see, I couldn't possibly come without Deborah, and she couldn't come, because she has a mummy and daddy who couldn't do without her."

"But think how lovely it would be," said the fairy with the star in her hair. "You would have a beautiful dress like mine, with pink and yellow frills, and you would drink honey out of rose petals, and we should powder your fur with star-dust so that you would shine in the dark. You would have such a lovely time with us you would never miss Deborah at all."

"Oh, but I should! I know I should!" said Teddy Robinson. "You see, we are very special to each other. And, anyway, I promised her I would stay sitting here until she came back."

Then all the fairies joined hands in a circle and began to dance round and round Teddy Robinson, singing in tiny little teasing voices:

"Teddy bear,
fat and fair,
don't be a quite-contrary-bear.
Fly with us,
as free as air;
be a fairy, teddy bear."

But Teddy Robinson just said, "No. No. I'm going to stay sitting here like I promised Deborah."

Then the fairies danced faster and faster round him until their feet weren't even touching the ground; and they all spread out their wings most beautifully until Teddy Robinson thought it was quite the prettiest sight he had ever seen.

He began to have a little think about how pretty he too would have looked with a pair of fairy wings.

He began to feel as light as a feather. He forgot about his fat tummy and his big feet, and soon he felt just as if he were floating through the air.

And the fairies, as if they knew all about his little think, began to sing again:

How pretty he too would have looked with a pair of fairy wings

"Airy bear,
fairy bear,
floating lightly in the air,
borne aloft on fairy wings,

while fairies dance in fairy rings,
and every dancing fairy sings,
'Oh, airy, fairy bear!' "

Then, just as Teddy Robinson was thinking he might really take off without meaning to, he heard footsteps coming down the grassy path, and there was Deborah running up to him with the basket in her hand. And in less than a second every single fairy had flown away! Deborah never saw even the end of a fairy's wing. All she saw was her dear old Teddy Robinson sitting just where she had left him by the edge of the grassy path.

"You *are* a good boy," she said, as she picked him up and hugged him. "You stayed sitting down just as you promised. I knew you wouldn't run away."

"So did I," said Teddy Robinson, "and I knew I wouldn't walk away, or crawl away, or hop or skip or jump away. But what I *didn't* know was that I should jolly nearly fly away!"

And then while they picked enough blackberries to fill the basket right to the top Teddy Robinson told Deborah all about what had happened to him in the little green lane.

"They were beautiful," he said. "They were just like in Auntie Sue's book, and they did have wings, and they did wear garlands, and they did dance all in a ring."

"I wish I had seen them too," said Deborah.

"So do I," said Teddy Robinson. "But I'll share it with you. You always give me half of anything nice, so I'll give you half of my seeing the fairies, and we'll keep it as a special secret, all to ourselves."

And that is the end of the story about
Teddy Robinson and the fairies.

9

Teddy Robinson
and Guy Fawkes

One wintry afternoon Teddy Robinson was sitting under the dining-room table. He was all alone. Deborah had been playing houses with him until Mummy had sent her off to Andrew's house to invite him to her party on Saturday.

Teddy Robinson knew all about the party. He was looking forward to it a lot, because it was going to be a fireworks party, and Teddy Robinson loved things that went off with a bang. He began singing a little song about it to himself while he waited for Deborah to come back.

> "Fireworks are coming,
> hooray, hooray.
> Fireworks are coming
> on Saturday.
> Hold your ears

and hide your eyes.

BANG, BANG, BANG!

What a nice surprise!"

Teddy Robinson stopped singing and listened. He could hear Mummy and Daddy talking together in the kitchen.

"Where's Deborah?" said Daddy. "I thought we might make a guy. Have you got some old clothes and newspapers?"

"Oh, yes," said Mummy. "Deborah's gone to Andrew's house. I expect she's stayed to play with him. But let's go and see what we can find."

"Now, I wonder whatever they're talking about," said Teddy Robinson to himself. But he couldn't guess, because he didn't know what a guy was.

For a long time he could hear them talking and laughing together in the kitchen, but after a while he got tired of wondering what they were doing and dozed off to sleep instead.

He woke up with a start. Someone had just opened the door. Teddy Robinson peeped out from under the table and saw Daddy coming in with the funniest-looking man he had ever seen. Daddy sat the funny-looking man down on the floor and propped him up against the table-leg.

"There you are, old boy," he said. "You just wait till Deborah sees you!" Then he went out again and shut the door.

Teddy Robinson had a good look at the funny man.

He was wearing a very old coat of Daddy's, and a very old hat of Mummy's, and some very old leggings of Deborah's. His hair, sticking out from under Mummy's old hat, looked as if it was made of straw, and he had a funny, laughing face which looked just as though it had been painted on cardboard.

"Whoever are you?" said Teddy Robinson.

The funny man looked sideways at him. Then he laughed, and a strange noise of rustling newspapers came from inside his jacket.

"Fancy not knowing who *I* am!" he said.

"*I'm* Guy Fawkes, sir.
How do you do?

I'm Guy Fawkes, sir.
Who are you?"

"Whoever are you?"

"I'm Teddy Robinson. How do you do? May I ask what you're doing here? And why are you wearing my family's clothes?"

"Your family was kind enough to lend them to me," said Guy Fawkes. "I've come for the party."

"But the party isn't until Saturday," said Teddy Robinson.

"I know," said the guy; "but I like to be ready in plenty of time."

"I never heard of anyone coming to a party two whole days early," said Teddy Robinson. "Where are you going to stay?"

"Here, of course," said the guy. "It's only two days to wait. A short life but a merry one, eh? Ha, ha, ha!"

He laughed again with a great crackling of newspapers, and his hat slipped a little bit sideways on his head.

Teddy Robinson couldn't see anything to laugh at. He didn't much like the idea of this funny-looking man coming to live in his house. But the guy seemed to be a jolly fellow, so Teddy Robinson tried to be friendly and make him feel at home.

"We're going to have a lovely lot of fireworks on Saturday," he said.

"Good," said the guy. "There's nothing I like better. And will there be a lot of children here?"

"Oh, yes," said Teddy Robinson. "Deborah's gone

to invite one of them now. I expect she'll be home soon."

And at that minute Deborah came running in from Andrew's house. When she saw the guy sitting on the dining-room floor she laughed and clapped her hands.

"Daddy told me he was here," she said.

Teddy Robinson said, "This is Mr Spoons. He says he's come to stay. He came while you were out."

Deborah laughed more than ever.

"He's not Mr Spoons," she said, "he's Mr Fawkes, and he hasn't come to stay. He's come to be burnt on the bonfire."

Teddy Robinson was very surprised to hear Deborah say this. It didn't seem at all a polite thing to say about a visitor. But the guy didn't seem to mind. He just went on smiling all the time.

When bedtime came Teddy Robinson was very glad to find that the guy wasn't going to share their bed with them. He was quite happy to be left in the kitchen, propped up in a corner by the back door.

So Teddy Robinson was able to ask Deborah if it was really true that he was going to be burnt on the bonfire at the party.

"Oh, yes," said Deborah. "That is what guys are for. Aren't we lucky to have such a fine one?"

But Teddy Robinson was beginning to feel rather sorry for the guy.

All the next day the guy stood in the corner of the kitchen, grinning happily at every one as they came in and out. Teddy Robinson had a little talk with him once when they were left on their own.

"Do you like being you?" he asked. "You smile such a lot anybody'd think you enjoyed it."

"Oh, but I do," said the guy. "Don't you like being you?"

"Yes, thank you," said Teddy Robinson. "I like it very much. I was only thinking . . ." But he didn't know how to finish what he was saying, because he was thinking about what was going to happen to the guy on Saturday.

"I was thinking about the fireworks party," he said.

"Do you like being you?"

"So was I," said the guy. "I'm looking forward to it no end—aren't you?"

"Well, yes, I am," said Teddy Robinson; "but somehow I didn't expect a guy to. I saw one today at the shops being wheeled in a push-chair by a little boy, and I thought he looked rather sad."

"Oh, those guys in push-chairs!" said the guy. "I don't even count them; they're hardly guys at all. They haven't even got enough stuffing in them to sit up straight. And no wonder they look sad! They have to sit there for hours while the boys shout, 'Penny for the guy, mister!' Well, no decent guy would like to sit there listening to children begging for him, would he? Surely you don't think I look like one of them, do you?"

"Oh, no," said Teddy Robinson; "I think you're the finest guy I ever met, I really do."

Saturday came at last, and everybody was busy getting ready for the party. Deborah counted the fireworks over and over again. Mummy was busy making toffee-apples and scrubbing big potatoes to roast in the bonfire. Daddy made a huge pile of wood and old boxes down at the bottom of the garden.

But Teddy Robinson hung around feeling rather sad, and getting more and more worried about the guy. Did he know about the bonfire yet? He said he was looking forward to the party, so he *couldn't* know.

I wonder if I ought to tell him, thought Teddy Robinson.

"Why are you looking so sad?" asked Deborah. "Aren't you looking forward to the fireworks?"

"I think perhaps I won't go to the party, after all," said Teddy Robinson.

Just then Daddy came tramping in from the garden.

"Do take the guy outside," said Mummy. "He's in my way here."

So Daddy carried the guy outside and propped him up against the wall by the dustbins.

"I want to go out there with him," said Teddy Robinson.

"All right," said Deborah, and she took him out and sat him beside the guy on one of the dustbins.

The guy leaned up against the wall and looked down at Teddy Robinson with a great big, jolly smile.

"Well, well," he said, "it's the great day at last! Why so sad? Aren't you looking forward to the party?"

"Not much. I don't think I'm coming."

"Of course you're coming!" said the guy. "Look

142

here, I've just thought of something! Are you going to have a bonfire of your own?"

"How do you mean?" said Teddy Robinson.

"Well, they're not going to burn you on *my* bonfire, are they? It wouldn't be fair. There isn't room for two of us, and I don't want to share my bonfire with anybody."

"I'm not going to be burnt on any bonfire," said Teddy Robinson.

"Oh, bad luck!" said the guy. "No wonder you look sad!"

"But I don't *want* to be burnt on a bonfire," said Teddy Robinson. "Do you mean you really don't mind?"

"What a funny chap you are!" said the guy. "Why, I've been looking forward to it ever since I came. Every guy does. It's the big minute of his life. When the flames go shooting up all round me, and I start crackling and burning, I shall be the finest sight in the garden. Are you sure you're not jealous? You *must* come and watch me, or I shall know you're jealous, and that will spoil my finest minute."

Teddy Robinson was so pleased to hear the guy say this that he began looking forward to the party all over again.

"Of course I'll come," he said. "I wouldn't miss it for anything."

"That's a good fellow," said the guy.

So at half-past four, when all the children came, Teddy Robinson was just as excited as Deborah.

As soon as it was dark and tea was over they all put on their coats and ran out into the garden. Teddy Robinson, with a scarf tied round his neck, sat on the step by the garden door. Deborah gave him a sparkler all his own. He was very pleased.

"But I won't hold it," he said. "It might burn my paws."

So Deborah stuck the sparkler into some earth in a flower-pot and put it in front of him on the step.

"There," she said, "that is your very own firework."

"Will you light it before you burn the guy?" said Teddy Robinson. "I'd like him to see it before he goes."

"Yes," said Deborah. "Let's go and have a look at him now."

So they went down the garden to have a last look at the guy before Daddy set light to the bonfire.

He was standing right on top of the pile, smiling all over his face and staring up at the stars.

— smiling all over his face and staring up at the stars —

"Hallo," said Teddy Robinson. "I've just come to say good-bye. And I wanted to tell you, I've got a firework all of my own. Watch out for it.

It'll be the very first sparkler."

"I'll watch!" said the guy. "Jolly good show!" Then, as the other children all crowded round to admire him, the guy lurched a little sideways and whispered:

"Jolly nice of you to come and watch me, old boy. Never mind—your turn will come one day."

"Now stand back, all of you!" said Daddy. "I'm just going to light the bonfire."

"Wait!" cried Deborah. "Teddy Robinson's got to have his sparkler first. I promised him."

All the children ran to the step and stood round waiting to see Teddy Robinson's firework lighted. He felt very proud. But when it suddenly burst out spluttering he was so surprised that he rolled over backward and fell off the step. Deborah sat him up again, and he watched proudly until the last little silver star had died away. Teddy Robinson thought it was the finest firework he had ever seen.

After that Daddy lit the bonfire, and while the flames crept slowly upward he let off rockets, and Catherine-wheels, and jumping crackers; and all the children shouted "O-o-o-oh!" every

the finest firework he had ever seen

time a new one went off.

The bonfire roared and blazed and crackled at the end of the garden. Teddy Robinson could see the guy's proud and happy smile lit up by the bright flames until at last he was all burnt up.

The fireworks went *Bang, Crackle, Swish, Pop,* until Teddy Robinson could hardly hear himself thinking. And so many coloured stars and flares went shooting up into the sky that he didn't even know which way his eyes were looking.

147

Soon the garden was filled with the most delicious smell of gunpowder, and much later on with an even more delicious smell of roast potatoes. It was a wonderful party. It seemed to go on for hours and hours.

When at last it was over and the children had all gone home Deborah came to fetch Teddy Robinson to bed. She found him lying flat on his back on the step, staring up at the sky, and singing softly to the stars:

"Splutter, splutter, sparkle,
what a jolly sight!
Did you see my firework
exploding in the night?

"Splutter, crackle, BANG,
from six o'clock till nine,
fifty million fireworks,
but none as fine as mine!"

Soon Teddy Robinson was tucked up in bed beside

Deborah, his sleepy head still full of swishing stars and surprises.

He was just dropping off to sleep when he suddenly remembered the very last thing the guy had said to him, "Never mind—your turn will come one day."

Teddy Robinson woke up with a start.

"It won't, will it?" he said out loud to Deborah.

"What won't, will it?" said Deborah sleepily.

"My turn won't come, will it?" said Teddy Robinson. "I won't be burnt on a bonfire, will I?"

"Good gracious, no!" said Deborah. "What ever made you think of that?"

And that is the end of the story about
Teddy Robinson and Guy Fawkes.

10

Teddy Robinson
is a Baby-sitter

One day Teddy Robinson was dozing on top of the toy-cupboard when Deborah suddenly ran into the room and began tying a large white handkerchief round his tummy.

"Hallo!" said Teddy Robinson, waking up, "what's this?"

Deborah fixed a smaller white handkerchief round his head and tied it in a knot behind.

"What am I going to be?" said Teddy Robinson. Deborah held him up to the looking-glass.

"What do you think you look like?" she asked.

"A nurse?" said Teddy Robinson. "Yes, I do look rather like a nurse. Is that what I'm going to be?"

"Not exactly," said Deborah, "but something very like it, and a cap and apron suit you very well. You're going to be a baby-sitter."

"*Am* I?" said Teddy Robinson. "Tell me about it."

"Yes, I do look rather like a nurse"

So Deborah told him how Mrs Green had come, bringing her new baby with her in a pram, and, as it was time for the baby's rest, she and Mummy had decided to put him in the front garden while they talked together indoors.

"And I suddenly thought what a good baby-sitter you would make," said Deborah, "so I came to fetch you. Do you think you will like it?"

"Yes," said Teddy Robinson, feeling rather pleased and proud, "but I'm not quite sure what I have to do."

"Just watch the baby, that's all," said Deborah.

"That will be very nice," said Teddy Robinson. "I know how to watch toast, but I've never watched a baby before. Yes, I'll enjoy that. I'm rather good at watching things."

Half-way down the stairs he suddenly said, "I say! You don't think I'm too fat, do you?"

"How do you mean?" said Deborah.

"Too fat to sit on a baby, I mean," said Teddy Robinson. "I should like to be a baby-sitter very much, but I'd be sorry if I squashed the poor little thing."

"Oh, no, that will be all right," said Deborah. "I don't think baby-sitters have to sit *on* the baby. It's good enough if they just sit *by* them."

So they went out into the front garden, and there was Mrs Green's baby, fast asleep in his pram under the hawthorn-tree, looking very quiet and happy. Deborah lifted Teddy Robinson up so that he could see over the edge of the pram, and he made soft, teddy-bear noises at the baby.

"That's right," said Deborah. "I'm sure you'll be

a very good baby-sitter." And she sat him down in the other end of the pram, then ran indoors to talk to Mrs Green.

Teddy Robinson liked being a baby-sitter very much. It was pleasant and peaceful in the garden, the birds sang in the trees, and the breeze fluttered his handkerchief cap. He began singing to himself softly:

"Underneath the hawthorn-tree
who should baby-sit but me?
Wise and willing,
neatly dressed,
watching baby have his rest.
Kind and cosy,
here I am,
baby-sitting in the pram."

There was a fluttering overhead, and a moment later a sparrow flew down and perched on the edge of the pram.

"Hallo, who have we here?" he chirped, looking

brightly at the baby with his head on one side.

"This is Mrs Green's baby," said Teddy Robinson proudly, "and I am the baby-sitter."

"Really?" said the sparrow. "Forgive my saying so, but I don't think you're sitting very well. My own babies have just hatched out nicely, but I don't think they would have if I hadn't sat on them a good deal better than that. How can you expect to keep him warm if you sit right at the other end of the nest?"

"Yes, but this baby isn't an egg," said Teddy Robinson. "I was told it was quite right to sit at this end."

"Oh," said the sparrow, "perhaps you're right. He's a nice-looking baby, I must say."

"Tell me," said Teddy Robinson, "—you have babies of your own, so you should know—why has he no fur on his head? He's quite a new baby, I know, and I'm sure he was an expensive one; it seems a shame his fur should have worn off already, doesn't it?"

The sparrow looked at the baby carefully.

"I think it's all right," he said. "It's probably meant

to be like that. My babies don't have feathers on when they're new, either."

"Is that so?" said Teddy Robinson. "My own fur is a little thin on top, but I shouldn't have thought it was because I was new. Perhaps it's different for teddy bears."

"I expect so," said the sparrow. "What a very nice nest you have here! My own nest is up in that tree. I almost think I should have preferred yours if I'd seen it first; that blanket looks so soft and warm. But, of course, a nest on wheels is rather a newfangled idea. I'm not sure that my wife would have liked it. Poor bird, she works very hard; I wish I could find some one as good as you to help her. I suppose you wouldn't like the job of baby-sitting for us some time?"

Teddy Robinson was about to say thank you, but he was afraid he would be rather too big to sit in a bird's nest, when the sparrow suddenly flew up into the tree, and at the same moment the Next Door Kitten came padding softly along the garden wall.

"Hallo," she said, "what are you doing there?"

"I'm baby-sitting," said Teddy Robinson.

"What a charming home you have for your baby," said the kitten, admiring the pram. "My mother has just had a new litter of kittens. I must tell her about this. It would be a delightful place for her to keep them in."

Teddy Robinson was just going to say no, that wouldn't do at all because the pram already belonged to Mrs Green's baby, when the kitten suddenly scrambled up the tree, and at the same moment the puppy from over the road came lolloping up the path, wagging his tail.

"Hallo," he said, "what are you doing up there?"

"I'm baby-sitting," said Teddy Robinson.

"Are you really? That's a jolly nice puppy-basket on wheels," said the puppy from over the road, and he stood up on his hind legs, trying to see inside the pram.

"Please don't do that," said Teddy Robinson. "I'm afraid you'll wake the baby."

Just then the puppy caught sight of the kitten half-way up the tree, and began barking loudly. The kitten scrambled higher up the tree and sat on a branch, hissing and spitting, and the sparrows (who thought the kitten was after their babies at the top of the tree) began chirping and twittering and flapping their wings.

Teddy Robinson said, "Hush!" and "Please be quiet," and "*Do* you mind not making so much noise?"; but no one took any notice of him. They went on barking, and hissing, and spitting, and cheeping, and twittering, and flapping, until at last he drew a deep breath and shouted at the top of his voice, "GO AWAY, ALL OF YOU! I won't have you all quarrelling and shouting like this!"

Then the kitten scampered away, the puppy ran out of the gate, the sparrows stopped cheeping, and it was quiet again in the garden.

"I should think so too," said Teddy Robinson to himself. "I never heard such a noise. It was enough to wake anybody's baby."

And, sure enough, at that moment the baby opened its eyes and mouth and began crying.

"Oh, dear," said Teddy Robinson, "please don't

cry! I don't know what to do to make you stop, but it does make me look such a silly baby-sitter if I can't."

But the baby went on crying.

After a while the sparrow flew down from the tree again. He perched on the edge of the pram and stared down into the baby's open mouth. Then he turned to Teddy Robinson.

"That baby's hungry," chirped the sparrow. "Look how wide open his beak is."

"Do you really think so?" said Teddy Robinson.

"That baby's hungry"

A yellow-hammer from a near-by tree suddenly called out, "A little bit of bread and no cheese!"

"No," said the sparrow, "what that baby needs is a nice little feed of worms. I'll go and see if I can find some." And he flew off.

The Next Door Kitten came walking along the wall again.

"*Mia-ow-ow!*" she said, "What a mewing! He's hungry."

"Do you really think so?" said Teddy Robinson.

"Yes," said the kitten, "what that baby needs is a nice little bowl of fish. I'll go and see if I've got any left." And she jumped down into the next-door garden.

"What that baby needs is a nice little bowl of fish"

The puppy from over the road came back.

"*Woof!*" he said. "What a terrible whining and howling!"

"I know," said Teddy Robinson, "I think he's hungry."

"Oh, no," said the puppy, "he's not hungry. He's probably teething. What that baby needs is a nice big juicy bone to help his teeth come through. I'll go and dig one up." And he went galloping away over the road into his own garden.

And still the baby went on crying.

Teddy Robinson sat in the pram feeling very muddled and worried. Every one had told him something different, and they all seemed perfectly sure they were right. Only Teddy Robinson didn't feel sure about anything at all. The baby was still crying, and he could hear the voices of the others from all around.

"A nice little feed of worms!" the sparrow was chirping from the garden bed.

"A nice little bowl of fish!" the kitten was mewing from the next-door garden.

"A nice big juicy bone!" the puppy was barking from over the road.

And, "A little bit of bread and no cheese!" called the yellow-hammer over and over again.

"Oh, dear!" said Teddy Robinson, "I wonder which of them is right. Or are they all right? I wish I knew."

An old lady came walking slowly up the road. She stopped at the gate when she heard the baby crying.

"Dear, dear, poor little thing!" she said to herself. "What that baby needs is a nice little lullaby—a soothing little song to send it to sleep. I'd stay and sing to it myself if I hadn't got to go home and get tea ready. Dear, dear, poor little thing!" And she went slowly on up the road, shaking her head.

"Why, of course!" said Teddy Robinson to himself. "Why ever didn't I think of it before?" And he began singing to the baby in a gentle, soothing growl:

161

"Hush-a-bye,
hush-a-bye,
this is Teddy's lullaby.
Fold your paws
and close your eyes,
no more growling,
no more sighs;
shut your mouth
and please don't cry,
Teddy R. is sitting by
singing you a lullaby,
hush-a-bye,
hush-a-bye . . ."

and by the time he had got as far as this the baby was fast asleep.

"There now," said Teddy Robinson, smiling to himself, "I wonder why I listened to all those others. *I'm* the baby-sitter, not them. Of course I should know how to send a baby to sleep."

And when Deborah came running out a moment later the garden was as quiet and peaceful as if the baby had never woken up at all.

"It's tea-time, Teddy Robinson," said Deborah. "Would you like to come in now?"

"Oh, yes," said Teddy Robinson, "that would be very nice. Baby-sitting is harder work than I thought. I shall be quite glad to sit down and have a rest."

And that is the end of the story about how
Teddy Robinson was a baby-sitter.

11

Teddy Robinson
Stops Growing

One day Teddy Robinson was watching Deborah digging in her garden. There was a nice fresh smell in the air, the sun shone warm on his fur, and he thought how nice it was to be out of doors again after the long, cold winter.

Soon he heard a rustling noise near by and saw that a large pile of leaves was moving. A moment later the garden tortoise poked his head out and looked round, blinking.

"Hallo," said Teddy Robinson. "Where have you been?"

"Merry Christmas," said the tortoise.

"Thank you," said Teddy Robinson, "but Christmas was over long ago."

"Happy New Year, then," said the tortoise.

"Thank you again," said Teddy Robinson, "but it isn't New Year either. I rather think this is spring."

"Ah, better still!" said the tortoise. "I always come up in spring. I went down under ground last autumn when the leaves fell off the trees—felt I couldn't stand the cold winter, you know."

"Oh, dear, then, I'm afraid you did miss Christmas!" said Teddy Robinson. "What a pity!"

"Never mind," said the tortoise, "we can't all have everything. You had your Christmas and I had my nice warm bed. Tell me, what's new? How is the old place?" He peered round the garden, blinking in the sunlight.

"My word!" he said, "that hedge has grown thick."

"Has it?" said Teddy Robinson. "I never noticed."

"Oh, yes," said the tortoise; "last year it hardly—I say! Who is that very large person digging over there?"

"That's not a large person," said Teddy Robinson. "That's Deborah. Does she know you're out yet?"

"Deborah?" said the tortoise. "Goodness me! I must go and see her." And he waddled off down the path.

Mummy came out into the garden.

"Oh, look! Dear old Tortle is back," she said. "Spring is really here. How good it is to see everything growing, and Tortle coming out again, and the days growing longer!"

She found a cabbage-leaf for Tortle, and Deborah filled a little dish with water for him to drink.

"That reminds me," said Mummy, "your daffodil needs watering, and so does Teddy Robinson's. Run and get them."

Deborah and Teddy Robinson each had a daffodil in a flower-pot. Auntie Sue had brought them at Christmas. For a long while Teddy Robinson had watched his carefully every day to see if he could see it growing, but lately he had forgotten all about it.

Deborah brought the pots out into the garden.

"Just look how tall they are!" she said. "Last time we looked they weren't nearly as big."

"Now, how did they do that?" said Teddy Robinson.

"Well, we watered them sometimes," said Deborah, "I think that helped. And when they were

"Now, how did they do that?"

new we put them in the dark in the cupboard, do you remember? Auntie Sue said that was the way to start them growing."

"And Auntie Sue is coming to tea to-day," said Mummy. "I must get back to my baking."

Deborah carried the daffodils back into the house, and Teddy Robinson sat in the sun and sang to himself because it was spring and everything was so jolly.

In a minute the puppy from over the road came

galloping up. He was so pleased to see Teddy Robinson that he bowled him over like a ball, then ran round him in circles.

"Hallo, little teddy bear," he said. "Sorry if I upset you. How do you like my new collar?"

Teddy Robinson tried to look as if he had been rolling in the grass on purpose.

"I'm not a little teddy bear," he said, "I'm a good middling-sized bear. But let's see your new collar."

The puppy stood still, and Teddy Robinson saw that he was wearing a big brown collar with gold studs all round it.

"That is very fine," he said, "but what's happened to the little red one you used to wear?"

"Grown out of it!" said the puppy proudly. "This is my first grown-up collar. They say I'm growing fast. Isn't it fun! You're not growing much, are you?"

"Perhaps not at the moment," said Teddy Robinson. "I've too much else to think about. I expect I shall soon, though."

"I wonder you don't start now," said the

puppy. "Where is everybody?"

"Indoors," said Teddy Robinson. "Mummy's baking."

"Oh, is she?" said the puppy. "That's interesting." And he wandered off towards the house, sniffing the air.

Teddy Robinson lay in the long grass and thought hard.

"Everything seems to be growing," he said to himself. "The hedge is growing thicker, the days are growing longer, the daffodils are growing taller, and now even that pup says he's growing bigger. Well, I only hope I'm growing too."

"But you're not, you know," said Tortle. "Last year I could reach the top of your foot with my nose, and this year I find I still can."

"Dear me!" said Teddy Robinson. "Oh, dearie me!"

"Don't worry," said the tortoise. "Life is sweet. Spring is here, and time goes on and on, and round and round. Life is very sweet, teddy bear; why should you bother about growing?"

"I wouldn't, only every one else seems to," said Teddy Robinson.

When Deborah came out again he said, "What would happen if you put me in a flower-pot and watered me?"

"You'd get very wet," said Deborah.

"Is that all? Wouldn't anything else happen?"

"No. What else could happen?" said Deborah. She had forgotten about the daffodils now and thought it was a very silly-bear question.

After a while Teddy Robinson said, "You know, I've started thinking about cupboards now."

"Have you?" said Deborah. "What sort of cupboards?"

"Dark cupboards," said Teddy Robinson.

"How many of them?" said Deborah.

"One would do," said Teddy Robinson.

"What for?" said Deborah.

"For me to sit in," said Teddy Robinson.

"What *do* you mean?" said Deborah.

"I was only thinking how much I should like to sit in a dark cupboard for a little while," said Teddy Robinson.

"What a funny old boy you are!" said Deborah. "I suppose you can sit in a dark cupboard if you want to. But I won't sit with you. I don't like dark cupboards."

"Oh, I do!" said Teddy Robinson. "Can I sit in one now?"

"Yes, I suppose so, if you really mean it," said Deborah. So she carried him indoors and put him in the cupboard under the stairs on top of a pile of old newspapers.

"Is that what you really want?" she asked.

"Yes, thank you," said Teddy Robinson. "Good-bye."

"Good-bye," said Deborah. "When shall I fetch you?"

"I really ought to stay here about six weeks," said Teddy Robinson, "but dinner-time will do."

So Deborah shut the door, and Teddy Robinson sat quite still in the dark and waited to begin growing. The daffodils had been no bigger than bulbs when they were first put in the cupboard, and now they were as tall as he was.

"So there's no knowing *how* big I may grow," said Teddy Robinson to himself, "because I was quite a good middling-sized bear when I came in."

To help himself start growing he began singing about all the biggest things he could think of:

> "Elephants,
> and giants,
> and hippopotami,
> tall giraffes
> with heads so high
> they nearly reach the sky . . ."

and soon he felt a sort of tingling in his fur.

Hooray, he thought, I'm sure I'm beginning to grow. His arms began to feel like large furry sausages, and his legs began to feel like huge furry tree-trunks.

"Yes," he said, "I'm sure I'm growing bigger and bigger. I wonder how long it will be before my head touches the ceiling. Perhaps I shall grow too big for the cupboard and burst right out of it."

He began singing again, in a big, booming voice:

"Elephants,
and giants,
and hippopotami
can never be
as big as me
or half as tall as I."

And then at last Deborah came, and Teddy Robinson was brought out into the daylight again. But she didn't say, "Oh, Teddy Robinson, how big you've grown!" All she said was, "I'm sure you don't want to sit in this dusty old cupboard any more. Let's go out in the garden."

Teddy Robinson was surprised.

"Don't I look any different?" he asked as they went out.

"Yes," said Deborah, "you've got a cobweb on your head. Oh—and there's a spider running about in your fur!"

She shook it out on to the grass.

"Is that all?" said Teddy Robinson.

"Yes," said Deborah, wiping away the cobweb. "Now you look just as usual." And she kissed him on the nose.

Teddy Robinson was disappointed not to have grown big enough to surprise everybody, but he still thought he must have grown a *little* bit; so after a while he said, "Do you remember when you used to stand me up against the wall to see how tall I was?"

"Yes," said Deborah.

"My nose used to come just above your knee, didn't it?"

"I believe it did," said Deborah.

"Well," said Teddy Robinson, "I think perhaps it may come a *little* higher now. Shall we try and see?"

So Deborah stood him up against the wall.

Teddy Robinson stared hard at Deborah's legs, but his nose came quite a bit *lower* than her knees!

"Are you standing on tiptoe?" he asked.

"No," said Deborah. "Truly I'm not."

174

"And are you sure I'm standing, not sitting?"

"Quite sure," said Deborah, stepping backward to look.

"Well I never!" said Teddy Robinson, and he was so surprised he fell flat on his face.

Deborah stood him up against the wall again.

"How high do you come up?" she said. "Let's see."

"*Below* your knees," said Teddy Robinson. "Just look!"

"How high do you come up?"

"So you do!" said Deborah. "How funny I never noticed! It almost seems as if you're growing *smaller*, doesn't it?"

"That's just what I was thinking," said Teddy Robinson sadly. "I'm afraid you're right."

When Deborah was called in to change her dress and have her hair brushed Teddy Robinson stayed under the apple-tree. He didn't feel like having his fur brushed for Auntie Sue, and, anyway, he was afraid his best purple dress wouldn't fit him any more now that he was growing so small.

"I wish I'd never sat in that silly cupboard," he said. "How was I to know it would make me grow smaller?"

He began singing to himself in a small, sad voice:

"The days are growing longer,
the grass is growing high,
it seems to me
the apple-tree
can nearly reach the sky.

The plants are growing bigger,
and Debbie's growing tall;
how sad to be
a bear like me
who's only growing small."

There was a sudden muffling and scuffling, and the puppy from over the road came bounding across the grass, carrying something rather large in his mouth.

"What have you got there?" said Teddy Robinson.

The puppy dropped what he was carrying on to the flower bed. Then he looked quickly over his shoulder, licked his lips, and said, "Chocolate cake. Like a piece?"

"Chocolate cake. Like a piece?"

"No, thank you. Where did you get it from?"

"Off your kitchen table," said the puppy. "It *is* fun—I find I can just reach it if I stand on my back legs! I never used to be able to. Can you?"

"No," said Teddy Robinson.

"You know what?" said the puppy, gobbling cake, "I think I'm growing bigger and you're growing smaller."

"I know," said Teddy Robinson, "but don't let's talk about it. That cake was for tea. Are you going to eat it all?"

"I thought I'd eat half and bury the rest," said the puppy. "It might come in handy later."

Teddy Robinson watched while the puppy scrabbled in the earth and buried the other half of the cake.

"It might grow if you leave it long enough," he said. "A chocolate-cake-tree would be nice, wouldn't it?"

A motor-car horn hooted loudly at the front gate.

"That will be Auntie Sue," said Teddy Robinson. The puppy dived under the hedge out of sight, and a moment later Auntie Sue and Deborah came into the garden.

"How big you're growing, Debbie!" said Auntie Sue. "And how is dear Teddy Robinson? Oh, there he is, just the same as ever!" she said, as she caught sight of him sitting under the apple-tree.

Well, anyway, she doesn't seem to notice that I'm growing smaller, thought Teddy Robinson.

Mummy came out from the garden door.

"Does anyone know what's happened to my chocolate cake?" she called. "I left it on the kitchen table and now it's gone. It's most peculiar. Where can it be?"

But, of course, nobody knew except Teddy Robinson, and he didn't say.

"Perhaps you forgot to make it," said Deborah.

"But I'm sure I made it," said Mummy. "I remember putting it out to cool. And now there's nothing for tea."

"Never mind," said Auntie Sue. "Let's all drive into town and buy some buns, then we can take our tea into the woods. It's a lovely day for a picnic."

179

The puppy crawled out, wagging his tail.

"That will be fun!" he whispered to Teddy Robinson. "I love a picnic. All the food is on the ground, and you can taste a bit of everything while people are talking."

"Oh, here's Pup!" said Deborah. "Can he come too?"

"Goodness, no!" said Auntie Sue. "He's far too big for my little car. He has grown much bigger since I last saw him!"

"What about Teddy Robinson?" said Deborah. "Can he come?"

"Yes, of course," said Auntie Sue. "There will always be enough room for Teddy Robinson."

"I'm glad I'm not too big to fit into the car, anyway," said Teddy Robinson, as Deborah quickly changed his trousers for his best purple dress, "but I hope I shan't grow *very* much smaller."

"Oh, I forgot to tell you!" said Deborah. "It's all right about your growing smaller. I asked Mummy and she says you're not. It's only me growing bigger. Mummy says people stop growing when they're big enough. She has."

The puppy watched sadly as they all climbed into the car. Teddy Robinson felt quite sorry for him.

"Never mind, you've still got the cake," he whispered.

"Why, so I have!" said the puppy. "I'd forgotten all about it!" And he galloped off quite happily to dig it up again.

"I *am* glad I've stopped growing," said Teddy Robinson to Deborah as they set off. "If I'd grown any bigger I shouldn't have been able to come on the picnic; and if I'd grown any smaller I shouldn't be able to wear my best purple dress. As it is, I seem to be exactly right after all. I think I'll stay this size always."

And that is the end of the story about how Teddy Robinson stopped growing.

12

Teddy Robinson is
Taken for a Ride

One day Teddy Robinson and Deborah went down
to the sweetshop at the bottom of the road.

"Can I sit on the ledge outside and wait for you?"
said Teddy Robinson. "I like watching the people."

"All right," said Deborah, and she propped him
up with his back to the window. Then she went in.

She propped him up with his back to the window.

Teddy Robinson sat up very straight and proud, and thought how clever he was not to topple over. Soon a dog came sniffing round the door. It looked up at him and barked.

"Is that your shop?"

"No," said Teddy Robinson, "but that's my little girl inside. She's buying bull's-eyes."

"Why do you look so proud if it's not your shop?" said the dog. "Pride comes before a fall, you know."

And at that minute Teddy Robinson toppled forward on his nose and fell over on to the pavement.

The dog ran off, thinking Teddy Robinson was after him, and for a while no one else saw what had happened. Then a lady came by and picked him up.

"Is that your pram?" she said, and popped him into a baby's pram close by. Then she walked on.

"No, it isn't," said Teddy Robinson, "but I'm glad she thought it was. It's a very nice pram."

Just then a lady hurried out of the shop, threw a magazine on top of him, looked at the baby asleep in the other end, and started to push the pram.

"Goodness gracious," said Teddy Robinson under

the magazine, "I do believe I'm being carried away in front of my very eyes. What ever next?" And he wondered what Deborah would say.

After a while the pram stopped. The lady lifted the magazine off Teddy Robinson, and he saw that they were by a seat in the park. Then the lady saw him.

"Hallo, who ever put you in here?" she said.

Teddy Robinson couldn't tell her because he didn't know the name of the lady who had picked him up, so he looked friendly and said nothing.

The lady lifted him out and looked at him carefully. She saw that his fur was worn a little thin in places, and that one of his ears had once come off, and been sewn on again by hand. And she saw that his braces were fastened to his trousers with real buttons. But there wasn't a name tape anywhere.

"Someone cares for you, I can see that," she said. And she sat him on the seat, hoping that whoever he belonged to would come and find him there.

When the lady had pushed the pram away,

Teddy Robinson sat by himself, and thought how lucky he was to be a cared-for bear. And because it was pleasant in the park, and a bright sunny morning, he sang to himself to pass the time away,

> "It's nice to be
> a cared-for bear—
> not one you pick up anywhere.
> My fur is wearing,
> here and there,
> but little signs
> of wear and tear
> will show in any well-loved bear.
> And Mummy,
> when she's time to spare,
> will always do a small repair.
> She even made
> the clothes I wear,
> my dress, and trousers (just one pair),
> each button sewn
> with loving care—
> I really am a lucky bear!"

Just then, the park keeper came along. He stopped to pick up a newspaper that someone had dropped, then he saw Teddy Robinson on the seat.

"Well, I don't know!" he said, picking him up too. "The things people leave lying about!"

He can't mean me, thought Teddy Robinson. I wasn't lying about. I was sitting up properly.

The park keeper carried him and the newspaper along to a basket, which was fixed to a post by the side of the path. He put the newspaper in, then sat Teddy Robinson down on top of it. Then he went away.

Teddy Robinson sat inside the basket (which was made of wire and painted green) and felt very pleased.

"I think that man knew I was rather special," he said to himself, "so he's given me a seat all to myself. It's very nice, a splendid position. Most kind of him."

After a while a cat came along. She stopped when she saw Teddy Robinson and walked all round the post, looking up at the basket and the notice on it. Then she sat down and stared.

Teddy Robinson bowed slightly, inside the basket, and said, "Good day."

"Miaou are you?" said the cat.

"Miaou are you?"

"Very well, thank you," said Teddy Robinson.

"Is that your name?" said the cat, looking at the notice. "Am I speaking to Mr Litter?"

"Oh, no. My name is Teddy Robinson."

"Ow," said the cat, in a miaouly sort of voice, "And miaou are your kittens?"

"What kittens?" said Teddy Robinson.

"Isn't there a litter of kittens in that basket?"

"No, of course not," said Teddy Robinson.

"Miaou?" said the cat. "Ow very strange! That notice says LITTER HERE. But if you're not Mr Litter, and there isn't a litter of kittens in the basket, then that notice is all wrong."

Teddy Robinson was quiet, thinking.

"Not that *I* care, I only wondered," said the cat, and she stalked away, shaking the dust off her paws.

Then a big dog came bounding along. He stopped and sniffed round Teddy Robinson's feet.

"Don't do that," said Teddy Robinson.

"Why not?" said the dog. "I always sniff here."

"It isn't for you. It's a cat's basket," said Teddy Robinson.

"Oh, no, it's not!" said the dog. "It's for waste-paper, and apple cores, and ice-cream cartons."

"Rubbish," said Teddy Robinson.

"That's right," said the dog. "That's why I like it. Fancy wanting to sit in a litter-bin!"

Just then a man came round the corner, whistling.

"That's my master," said the dog. "Look, he has just found a baby's glove. I bet you he'll put it in there with you. Cat's basket indeed!"

The man came up, carrying a little woollen glove. He looked at Teddy Robinson as if he was surprised to see him sitting there. Then he dropped the glove on to his lap, and walked on.

"I told you so!" barked the dog, and ran off after him.

This was a nice little seat until I knew it was a rubbish basket, thought Teddy Robinson sadly. Now I'm beginning to feel rather like rubbish myself.

A bird flew down, perched on a near-by branch, and cocked its head cheekily at him.

"Is that your nest?" he chirped. "It's just the place for you, isn't it?"

"No," said Teddy Robinson, "it's a rubbish basket."

"And very nice too," said the bird. "I say, is that your glove? If so, I can tell you who's got the other one. She's just coming along now."

At that minute a girl came round the corner, pushing a baby in a push-chair. The bird flew away.

The girl walked slowly, looking from side to side of the path as she went. Then she looked up and saw Teddy Robinson in the basket. She came over to him.

"Oh, look!" she said to the baby. "There's a funny old teddy bear in here! And he's got your glove! He must have been looking after it for you. Oh, I am so glad we've found it!"

She lifted Teddy Robinson out of the basket.

"Poor old thing," she said. "You are a bit shabby, but it's a shame to throw you away." And she put him in the push-chair with the baby.

"We must run now," she said. "We've been so long looking for that glove, Mummy will wonder where we are. And we haven't done the shopping yet."

Then she began to run, and the push-chair began to rattle, and Teddy Robinson began to bounce, and the baby began to laugh. And they all went rattling and bouncing and bumping along at a great speed, out of the park and along the road.

—rattling and bouncing and bumping along at a great speed—

Soon they came to a corner that Teddy Robinson knew. It was his own road! And a minute later they drew up outside the very shop where Deborah had left him.

Quickly the girl got out her purse and shopping bag, and lifted the baby down. She propped Teddy Robinson up on the window ledge while she put the push-chair against the wall.

Just then the baby toddled off into the shop by himself. The girl didn't wait to pick Teddy Robinson up, but ran after the baby as fast as she could.

Teddy Robinson was very glad to find himself back where he had started! Feeling muddled and happy, and rather pleased with his adventure, he began singing a muddled and happy little song.

"Here I are, just as I were,
sitting on the sill.
Who would say I'd been away?
(I'm still just sitting still.)

A lady took me for a ride
(she really didn't should),
I landed in a litter-bin
(I thought I'd gone for good).

But someone kindly pulled me out,
and home to here we ran,
so here I are, just as I were,
right back where I began!"

Then, who should he see but Deborah, running down the road towards him.

"Oh, there you are, Teddy Robinson!" she said, picking him up and hugging him. "Do you know, I went all the way home without you! I *am* sorry I forgot you! What a dull time you must have had."

"Oh, no!" said Teddy Robinson.

"You are a good boy just to sit and wait," she said, "but I suppose you couldn't really do anything else, could you?"

"Oh, couldn't I?" said Teddy Robinson. "Shall I tell you a story about a teddy bear who got carried away in front of his very eyes, and a cat who thought his name was Litter, and a girl who was looking for a baby's glove?"

"Yes, tell me now," said Deborah.

So Teddy Robinson told her the story all the way home.

And that is the end of the story about how
Teddy Robinson was taken for a ride.

13

Teddy Robinson
and the Caravan

One day Teddy Robinson set off for a holiday in a caravan. He was so excited that he sang songs and asked questions all the way there.

"Is it a gipsy caravan?" he said. "Will it have a horse? Shall we be gipsies and follow the fair? Bless my braces, that's the life for a bear like me!"

But Daddy said, "No, it's a holiday caravan. It's a new one, and it lives behind a farm."

"I shall be a gipsy, all the same," said Teddy Robinson, "a gipsy bear with the wind in my hair—"

"You can't," said Deborah. "It's fur."

"I know, but it doesn't rhyme," said Teddy Robinson, and he sang loudly,

> "A bear doesn't care
> if it's fur or hair,
> as long as he's out in the open air.

I'll follow the fair,
so there, so there,
I'll still be a jolly old gipsy bear!"

But he forgot all about being a gipsy when he saw
the caravan. It was so full of surprises.

First Mummy lifted a flap from the wall, and it
turned into a table.

"Well, fancy that!" said Teddy Robinson.

Then Deborah pulled out a partition from inside
the wardrobe door, and it turned into a wall that
made the caravan into two rooms.

"Well, I never!" said Teddy Robinson.

Then Daddy turned a key in another wall and
said, "Now look at this!" And the whole wall came
outwards, and there inside was a big bed standing
on its head, all ready to be let down.

"Well, bless my braces!" said Teddy Robinson. "If
beds can come out of walls, and walls can come out
of wardrobes, anything can happen. Elephants can
come out of bird cages, and teddy bears can come
out of teapots." And he got so excited that he fell

over backward and landed in the big teapot that Mummy had just put on the table.

"Why, so they can!" said Daddy, and he put the lid on top of his head. "Now sing us a song!"

Teddy Robinson looked around at the things Mummy was laying out for tea, and sang,

> "Veal and ham,
> bread and jam,
> what a lucky bear I am!
> Cake I see,
> and eggs for tea,
> what a lucky bear I be!
> (but please don't pour the tea on me)."

"All right," said Mummy, laughing, "but get out quickly. I'm just going to make it. And then we must unpack and make up the beds."

After tea Teddy Robinson and Deborah ran around the fields until Mummy called them in to bed.

Soon they were tucked up on the seat under the window (which was now a cosy bed), enjoying all the bumps and bangs, as Daddy pulled out the partition and let down the big bed from the wall. Every time Mummy opened a locker, or Daddy fetched a water can, there was a great bumping and banging and clattering, and the whole caravan shook.

It wasn't a bit like going to bed at home.

Teddy Robinson sang a noisy little lullaby,

"Down comes the bed,
bumpety-bump,
out comes the wall,
thumpety-thamp,
clatter-and-clang

197

go bucket and can,
we're going to sleep
in a caravan!"

and he sang *biffety-bang, bumpety-bump, clattery-clang, thumpety-thump*, until Deborah fell asleep.

When at last everything was quiet and even Daddy and Mummy were asleep, he lay with his eyes wide open, staring at the sky through the open window, and listening to the country sounds. Corn rustled in the field, far away a dog barked, and a cow coughed in a field close by. Then he too fell asleep.

Once he half woke, hearing rustlings and scratchings quite near, and tiny voices squeaking. And once there was a harsh, shrill cry and he woke with a jump, feeling his fur stand up on end with fright. But Deborah slept on, so he went to sleep again too, and in the morning he had forgotten all about it.

Everything was a muddle in the morning. There were beds to make, blankets to fold, and breakfast to cook, all at the same time, and no room for anything. Teddy Robinson simply didn't know where he was.

First Daddy tripped over him on the floor, and popped him into a locker. Then Mummy threw blankets in on top and nearly smothered him. Then Deborah found him and put him in the big bed, but Daddy came and pushed it up into the wall, and turned the key.

By the time he was found again he was very grumpy, and all he would say was, "Let me out! Let me out!"

"But you are out," said Deborah.

"No, right out," said Teddy Robinson. "I've been locked in a locker, and folded in a bed (upside down inside a wall, and standing on my head), I'd rather be a gipsy bear and live outside instead."

"All right, let's go to the farm," said Deborah.

"Will there be cows?" said Teddy Robinson.

"Oh, yes," said Deborah, "chickens too."

"I don't think I will," he said. "Not that I'm *frightened* of cows, but I don't want to catch a cold.

I heard one of those cows coughing last night."

"You stay in bed then," said Deborah.

But Teddy Robinson still had a picture in his mind of being a gipsy bear, living out of doors, perhaps with a little camp fire to cook on.

He began mumbling to himself, in his own round-and-round sort of way, "I may be only a teddy bear, but I'm not a stay-in-beddy bear, I'm a jolly, rough-and-ready bear, I'd rather live in the open air, shutting me up just isn't fair, I'd *rather* be an outdoor bear, a carefree, open-airy bear, without a worry without a care, not even any clothes to wear . . ."

"Oh, all right," said Deborah, "but I won't have you sitting about with no clothes on. People will say I don't look after you properly. Anyway I thought you were afraid of catching cold?"

"Oh, yes, so I am!" said Teddy Robinson, "but the fresh air will soon cure that."

So half an hour later he was sitting on a grassy bank under the hedge, wearing his trousers and a red-and-white-spotted handkerchief round his neck. Beside him was a bundle of twigs, laid like a fire, and, best of all, on top of the twigs was an old tin kettle that Deborah had found in the ditch.

"You can have this for your own," she said, then she kissed him good-bye and ran off to the farm.

Teddy Robinson was very happy now. "This is the life for me," he said. "I feel better already. Fresh air and exercise, that's the thing. I can do without the exercise but I do like plenty of fresh air." And he took deep breaths, sitting up very straight with his tummy sticking out.

A fieldmouse ran past, looked up at him sideways, and disappeared over the bank. He sat very still and hoped she would come back. Soon she did. She came backwards and forwards many times, and at last she stopped, with her whiskers twitching.

"Good morning," said Teddy Robinson. "This is a fine life, isn't it?"

"It may be for you," said the fieldmouse rather sharply. "Camping is all very well for a city gentleman on his own, but it's very different with a family to feed. So much fetching and carrying!"

"This is a fine life, isn't it?"

"Dear me, I'm sorry," said Teddy Robinson, trying not to look so happy.

"It was easier when we lived in the cornfield," she said. "But now we live under a house—a very *nice* house, with very nice people—(we always choose very nice people)—it's just behind you."

"Oh, you mean our caravan!" said Teddy Robinson, very pleased. "But why do you live under us when you could live out in the cornfield?"

The fieldmouse shivered. "Haven't you heard?" she whispered. "Haven't you heard—in the night?"

202

Teddy Robinson suddenly remembered. "I did hear rustlings," he said. "Was that you? But you were squeaking as if you were frightened." Then he remembered the harsh, shrill scream. "What was it?" he asked, and his fur tingled as he remembered.

"It was Hooo-hooo, the owl," she said, in the smallest trembling whisper. "He's terrible. He hunts us in the night, flying over the fields and calling *Who-o-o? Who-o-o?* He means us, of course, and we all lie trembling in our beds. My children have such lovely bright eyes! He sees them shining in the moonlight, and then he swoops. That's why we're living under your house. Please don't tell!"

"Of course I won't," said Teddy Robinson.

When Deborah fetched him in at tea-time she was so full of the farm she could talk of nothing else.

"This holiday is doing you good," said Mummy, looking at her. "I do believe you're fatter and browner, and your eyes are brighter already."

"Thank you," said Teddy Robinson, bowing.

"Yes, you too," said Mummy. "It must be all that fresh air. I hope every day is as nice."

It was. Every day the sun shone. So every morning Deborah ran off to the farm, and Teddy Robinson sat in his own little camp on top of the bank, with his unlit fire and his old tin kettle.

His new friend, the fieldmouse (whom no one else knew about yet), soon became his old friend. And every day Teddy Robinson seemed to get fatter and browner, and his eyes seemed to shine more brightly.

Only at night, when he heard the scream of Hooo-hooo, the owl, he snuggled down in bed with Deborah and was glad he wasn't still camping out.

Then one day, near the end of the holiday, Daddy said the caravan was going to be moved nearer the farm for a while. Teddy Robinson ate no breakfast at all, he was so worried at this dreadful news.

As soon as he could, he told Mrs Fieldmouse.

"Oh! What ever shall I do?" she squeaked. "With no roof over our heads where should we be?"

"You'd still be in the field," said Teddy Robinson. "But I've an idea. Why don't you all move into my camp? The kettle would make a nice nest for you, and Hooo-hooo would never find you there."

"Oh, Mr Robinson Bear, how kind of you!" she cried. "What should I do without you? I'm sure we shall be most comfortable in your cosy kettle."

"But you must move quickly," he said. "The caravan is being towed away first thing tomorrow."

"Oh dear!" said Mrs Fieldmouse, "but it will take me all night to move my babies, one at a time. And I've only got two pairs of paws." She stared hard at Teddy Robinson. "Now you've got two fine, strong brown arms, Mr Robinson Bear. I wonder . . ."

"Oh, but I couldn't!" said Teddy Robinson. "My arms are all right, but I'm no good on my legs."

He tried to picture himself crawling about under the caravan, carrying away the baby fieldmice, but he knew it was impossible, and he felt ashamed.

Mrs Fieldmouse said, sniffing a little, "I'd have thought a big, strong gentleman like you (who's looking all the better for his holiday) would have been only too glad to help a poor, homeless family. Or don't city gentlemen care for children?"

"Oh, it's not that!" said poor Teddy Robinson.

He tried to picture himself crawling about under the caravan,

but he knew it was impossible.

"I love babies, truly I do."

Then he suddenly had an idea. "Mrs Fieldmouse," he said, sitting up straight and proud like a soldier, "you said the children's eyes shine brightly in the moonlight, and that's how Hooo-hooo sees them. Well, my eyes shine brightly too. And I'm much bigger. I myself will keep an eye open for him. I'll ask if I can stay out tonight. Just leave it to me."

"Oh, dear bear!" cried Mrs Fieldmouse. "What a good friend you are! Dear me! What ever shall I do when you've gone!" and she wiped away a tear.

"I'll be back," said Teddy Robinson. "I'll ask Deborah to bring me again before we go home."

"Oh, no! It's good-bye for ever, I know it is!" she cried, and she made tiny sniffling noises.

"Don't cry," said Teddy Robinson bravely. "I will come back if I don't get eaten. I hope I don't even more than you do."

Deborah wasn't at all sure whether she ought to leave Teddy Robinson out all night – not on purpose. But in the end she let him have his way.

So at bedtime, there he was, sitting all by himself up on the roof, waiting for it to get dark.

He heard first Deborah, then Mummy and Daddy go to bed. He listened to all the jolly bumps and bangs and clatters going on inside the caravan as usual, and wished he was down there too, safely tucked up with Deborah. Then he saw the farm lights go out and everything was quiet.

Soon the moon rose. Teddy Robinson waited with both eyes open, and, to keep his spirits up, sang a Brave Song,

"Hooo, Ha, Hooo,
I'm not afraid of you.
I know the terrible things you do,
you wicked old owl, *yahoo*, *yahoo*,
but I'm still not afraid of you, Hooo-hooo,
I'm still not afraid of you."

(but he was, of course).

Then in the distance, he heard a faint *Who-o*, *Who-o*, and the sound of large wings coming nearer. He felt as if he were frozen to the roof, and the fur on his ears stood up on end with fright.

With a great rustle of leaves, the owl landed in the top of a tree. "*Who-o-o?*" he called, in a horrible harsh scream. "*Who-o-o?*"

Teddy Robinson sat tight, his eyes shining brightly, and drew a big, brave breath. Then, as Hooo-hooo swooped down towards him, he shouted out at the top of his voice, "You! You! You!"

The owl swerved sideways with surprise. "Who-o are you?" he said, with a short, quavery squawk.

"I'm an owl-eater!" shouted Teddy Robinson.

*the fur on his ears
stood up on end with fright.*

"And I've been keeping an eye open for you!"

"Who?" squawked the owl faintly.

"Why, you! You! You silly old owl," said Teddy Robinson. "Be off before I eat you for my supper!"

"Ooo!" said the owl. And he circled round with a great flapping of wings and flew away.

It was nearly dawn when Teddy Robinson heard squeakings in the hedge, and knew that Mrs Fieldmouse had safely moved her family. He sighed with relief.

He thought of all the babies being put to bed

in his kettle, squeaking with excitement at moving in the night. He pictured them snuggling down together in their little brown fur coats. The thought made him drowsy. In another minute he was asleep.

When Deborah fetched him down in the morning, his fur was all wet with dew. He was longing to tell her all about Mrs Fieldmouse and the owl, but already the men had come to move the caravan.

As it was towed away across the field, he stared hard out of the back window, towards his little camp. He hoped Mrs Fieldmouse was watching, but it was too far away for him to see. He felt sad. His holiday was nearly over and he might never see her again.

Much later on, he was still sitting humped up by himself, when Deborah ran in, shouting, "Oh, Teddy Robinson! Guess what!" She hugged him till he squeaked. "Daddy's bought the caravan for our very own! We can come back here every summer!"

Teddy Robinson was pleased! He had to explore the caravan all over again then, because somehow it seemed different now he knew it was their own. And it looked nicer than ever!

Teddy Robinson did go to his little camp again. Deborah took him before they went home. He was afraid anyone so big might frighten the fieldmice, so he said, "Leave me alone a minute, and I promise I'll tell you all about it on the way home." So she did.

Teddy Robinson blew down the kettle spout and it made a hollow, roaring noise. He heard tiny scufflings down below, then a frightened bright eye gleamed up at him through the darkness.

"Hallo, Mrs Fieldmouse, are you there?" he said.

"Oh, Mr Robinson, dear bear, it's you!" squeaked Mrs Fieldmouse. "Oh, welcome to Cosy Kettle! Look, dear children, come and see who's here. It's our dear friend, Mr Robinson Bear!"

Teddy Robinson was pleased at such a welcome.

"I told you I'd come back!" he roared happily down the spout. "And what's more I'm coming back next summer, and the summer after, and the summer after that, and every summer for ever and ever hooray!"

211

And he got so excited, thinking about all the lovely summers to come, that he forgot he was on the edge of the bank and tumbled forward on his nose, and rolled head over heels all the way down to the bottom, where Deborah was waiting for him.

*And that is the end of the story about
Teddy Robinson and the caravan.*

14

Teddy Robinson
is a Polar Bear

One day Teddy Robinson sat under the apple-tree looking at a picture book. A little wind rustled the branches over his head, and soon one or two leaves came fluttering down around him.

"Dear me," said Teddy Robinson, looking upward, "this tree seems to be wearing out. Its leaves are falling off."

Then the wind blew a little stronger and one or two pages blew out of the book (which was an old one) and fluttered away on to the grass.

"There now," said Teddy Robinson, looking after them, "this book seems to be wearing out too. It's losing its leaves as well."

The wind blew stronger still, rustling the leaves and bending the long grass sideways.

"Br-r-r-r!" said Teddy Robinson; "it's cold. The wind's blowing right through my fur."

"It's getting thin," said a sparrow, flying past. "You should have chosen feathers like me. They wear better."

"Good gracious, do you mean I'm wearing out too?" said Teddy Robinson. But the sparrow had gone.

The garden tortoise came creeping slowly past.

"I'm quite worn out myself," he said. "I've been tramping round and round looking for a nice warm place to go down under. This pile of leaves looks as good as anywhere. Are you coming down under too, teddy bear? Winter's coming soon and the nights will be growing cold."

"Oh, no," said Teddy Robinson, "I always have a nice warm place down under Deborah's blankets when it's cold at nights."

"Oh, well, here goes," said the tortoise, and he began burrowing, nose first, deep into the pile of leaves.

"Anyway," said Teddy Robinson to himself as he watched the tortoise disappear, "I wouldn't care to spend the winter down there. Besides, I can't quite

214

remember what it is, but I believe there's something rather nice happens in winter-time. Something worth staying up for."

So the tortoise stayed buried, and the wind blew colder, and more and more leaves fell off the apple-tree. And because it had grown too cold to play in the garden any more, Teddy Robinson and Deborah played indoors or went for walks instead.

Then one day Teddy Robinson looked out very early in the morning, and saw that all the garden was white with snow. There was snow on the trees, and snow on the roofs of the houses, and thick snowflakes were falling in front of the window. He pressed his nose against the glass and stared out.

"Goodness gracious me," he said, "someone's emptied a whole lot of white stuff all over our garden. How different it looks!"

A robin flew down from a near-by tree, scattering snow as he flapped his wings. He hopped on to the window-sill and looked at Teddy Robinson through the window with his head on one side.

"Good morning!" he chirped. "What do you

"Good morning! What do you think of this?"

think of this? Got any crumbs?"

Teddy Robinson nodded at him behind the glass and said, "Good morning. I'm afraid I haven't any crumbs just now, but I'll ask Deborah at breakfast-time. What's it like out there?"

"Lovely," said the robin, puffing out his red waist-coat. "But you wouldn't like it. Snow is all right for white polar bears, but not for brown indoor bears. Well, I must be off now. Don't forget my crumbs!"

He flew away, and Teddy Robinson went on

watching the snowflakes falling outside the window and sang to himself:

> "There's snow in the garden,
> and snow in the air,
> and the world's as white
> as a polar bear."

When Deborah woke up, Teddy Robinson showed her the snow as proudly as if he had arranged it all himself (it felt like his snow because he had seen it first), and she was very pleased. As soon as breakfast was over she put out a saucer full of crumbs on the sill (because he had told her about the robin), and then she put on her coat and boots.

"I'm going to be very busy now," she said. "Andrew and I are going to dig away all the snow from people's gates."

"Can I come?" said Teddy Robinson.

Deborah looked out. "Yes," she said, "it's stopped snowing now. You can sit on the gate-post and watch us."

as proudly as if he had arranged it all himself.

So Deborah and Andrew started clearing the snow away from all the front gates while Teddy Robinson sat on his own gate-post and watched them. And after a while it began to snow again. Teddy Robinson got quite excited when he saw the big snowflakes settling on his arms and legs, and he began singing again, happily:

> "There's snow in the garden,
> and snow in the air,

and the world's as white
as a polar bear.

Snow on the rooftop,
and snow on the tree,
and now while I'm singing
it's snowing on me!"

"Hooray, hooray," he said to himself. "Perhaps if it snows on me long enough I shall be all white too. I should love to be a polar bear."

And it did. It snowed and snowed until Teddy Robinson was quite white all over, with only his eyes and the very tip of his nose showing through.

"I don't believe even Deborah would know me now," he said, chuckling to himself. And it seemed as if he was right, because when Deborah came running back for dinner Teddy Robinson kept quite still and didn't say a word, and she ran right past him into the house without recognizing him.

"This *is* fun!" said Teddy Robinson. "All this snow must be the nice thing I'd forgotten about, that happens in winter-time. It was worth staying up for." And he felt sorry for the poor old tortoise who was down at the bottom of the pile of leaves and missing it all.

How surprised Deborah will be when she comes back and finds I've turned into a polar bear, he thought.

But Deborah didn't come back because after dinner she made a snowman in the back garden and forgot all about him. Teddy Robinson didn't know this, but he was having such a jolly time being a polar bear all by himself on top of the gate-post that he didn't notice what a long time she was.

First the Next Door Kitten came picking her way along the wall, shaking her paws at every step. She looked at Teddy Robinson as if she didn't quite believe in him, and they had a little conversation.

"Who are you?"

"I'm a polar bear."

"Why aren't you at the North Pole?"

"I came to visit friends here."

"Oh!"

Then Toby the dog (who belonged to Deborah's friend Caroline) came galloping up. He was a rough and noisy dog who liked chasing cats and barking at teddy bears. The Next Door Kitten jumped quickly over the wall into her own garden, but Teddy Robinson kept quite still until Toby was sniffing round the gatepost. Then he let out a long, low growl.

Toby jumped and barked loudly. Teddy Robinson growled again.

"Who's that?" barked Toby.

"Gr-r-r, a polar bear. Run like mad before I catch you!"

Toby looked round quickly, but couldn't see anyone.

"Go on, *run*," said Teddy Robinson in his big polar bear's voice. "RUN!"

Toby didn't wait for any more. With a yelp which sounded more like Help! he ran off up the road as fast as he could go.

"Well, I'll never be frightened of *him* again," said Teddy Robinson.

Then the robin flew down from the hedge and

perched on the gate-post beside him and cocked a bright eye at him.

"Hallo," he chirped. "Who are you?"

"I'm a polar bear."

The robin looked at him sideways, hopped round to his other side, and looked again. Then Teddy Robinson sneezed.

"You're not," said the robin. "You're the brown bear who lives in the house. I saw you this morning. I told you then this snow isn't right for an indoor bear like you. You'll catch cold. But thanks for my crumbs. I'll look for some more at tea-time. I hope you'll be having toast? I like toast." And before Teddy Robinson could answer he had flown off again over the white roofs of the houses.

It grew very quiet in the road. People's footsteps made no sound in the snow and it seemed as if the world was wrapped in cotton wool. Teddy Robinson was beginning to feel cold. Soon one or two lights went on in the houses, and in a window opposite he could see a lady getting tea ready.

"I wonder if she is making toast," he said to

himself, and felt a little colder.

Then he began thinking about the tortoise tucked away in the big pile of leaves.

"He must be quite cosy down there," he said, and he thought of the leaves all warm and crunchy and smelling of toast, and almost wished he had gone down too.

"But of course, if I had, I should never have been able to be a polar bear sitting on a gate-post," he said; and to keep his spirits up he began singing a polar bear song:

> "Ice
> is nice,
> and so
> is snow.
> Ice
> is nice
> when cold winds blow———"

but the words were so cold that they made him sneeze again.

"Never mind," said Teddy Robinson bravely, "I'll think of something else. I'll make up a little song called The Polar Bear on the Gate-Post."

But it was hard to find anything to rhyme with gate-post, and the more he thought about it, the more he found himself saying "plate" instead of "gate," and "toast" instead of "post," so that in the end, instead of singing about a Polar Bear on a Gate-Post, he was singing about an Indoor Bear on a Plate of Toast, which wasn't what he'd meant at all.

"But it *would* be nice and warm sitting on a plate of toast," he said to himself. And then suddenly he thought, Of course! *That's* the nice thing that happens in winter-time. It's not snow at all. It's toast for tea!

And at that moment the robin came flying back chirping, "Toast for tea! Toast for tea! Is it ready?"

When he found the saucer empty on the window-sill and poor Teddy Robinson still sitting in the snow, with an icicle on the end of his nose, the robin was quite worried.

"They must have forgotten you," he said. "I'll remind them." And he flew up to the window and beat his wings hard on the glass. Then he flew back to Teddy Robinson.

Deborah came to the window and looked out.

"Oh, Mummy!" she called. "There's the robin, and he's sitting on—he's sitting on—why, it's Teddy *Robinson*, all covered in snow and looking just like a polar bear! And the robin's sitting on his head."

"Oh, don't they look pretty!" said Mummy. "Just like a Christmas card."

Then Teddy Robinson was brought in and made a great fuss of. And afterwards, while Mummy made

"just like a Christmas card—"

the toast for tea and Deborah put out fresh crumbs for the robin, he sat in front of the fire and bubbled and mumbled and simmered and sang, just like a kettle when it's coming up to the boil:

"Tea and toast,
toast and tea,
the tea for you
and the toast for me.
How nice to be a warm, brown bear
toasting in a fireside chair."

When bedtime came Teddy Robinson's fur was still not quite dry, so Mummy said he had better stay downstairs and she would bring him up later. So Deborah went off to bed, and Mummy went off to cook grown-up supper, and Teddy Robinson toasted and dozed in the firelight and was very cosy indeed.

Then Daddy came home, puffing and blowing on his fingers and stamping the snow off his shoes. He took a little parcel out of the pocket of his big overcoat and gave it to Mummy. Inside was a fairy doll, very small and pretty, with a white-and-silver dress, and a silver crown and wand.

"Oh, a new fairy for the Christmas-tree!" said Mummy, standing her upon the table. "How pretty! That is just what we need. Now come and have supper, it's all ready."

So Daddy and Mummy went off to their supper, leaving the fairy doll on the table and Teddy Robinson in front of the fire.

"A new fairy for the Christmas-tree," said Teddy Robinson to himself. "The *Christmas*-tree. I'd forgotten all about it," and his fur began to tingle. He suddenly remembered how the Christmas-tree looked, with toys and tinsel all over it, and little coloured lights, and a pile of exciting little parcels all round it. And he remembered himself, sitting close beside it in his best purple dress, trying to see if any of the parcels were for him, without looking as if he was looking. And then he remembered how there always was a parcel for him, and how it was always just what he wanted.

"Of course!" he said, "*that's* the nice thing that

happens in winter-time, that I'd forgotten about. It's not snow (though that's very nice), and it's not toast for tea (though that's nicer still), but it's Christmas, and that's nicest of all!"

There was a rustling over his head and the fairy doll whispered in a tiny little voice, "Would you like a wish, teddy bear? If you like you can have one now. It will be the very first wish I've ever given anyone."

Teddy Robinson said, "Thank you," then he thought hard, then he sighed happily.

"It seems a terrible waste of a wish," he said, "but I don't think I've anything left to wish for. I'll wish you and every one else a very merry Christmas."

And that is the end of the story about how Teddy Robinson was a Polar Bear.

The Teddy Robinson Storybook

Joan G. Robinson

"A friendly, free–and–easy bear,

a cosy, jolly, teasy bear

is always welcome

everywhere.

Fair and furry,

fat and free,

that's the kind of bear to be.

Like me."